THE WELL OF LETHE

A SPACE OPERA ADVENTURE EPIC

THE ECHO PLAGUE
BOOK 1

RICHARD PARRY

Find out more about Richard Parry at parrydox.com
Published by Richard Parry, New Zealand.

THE WELL OF LETHE

Korvus is a **Corrector**, an agent of the **machine god** that rules humanity. Armed with a weapon that fires black holes and a **faith forged in the fires of his own fallen world**, he descends into the deepest prison in the galaxy to eliminate a rogue AI.

His mission is to Correct the corruption—but he finds more than a heretical machine. **The Well of Lethe is already rotting from the inside**. The station is riddled with a horrifying biological plague, a parasite that creates perfect copies of its victims—**and can fool the Communion's most sacred security systems**.

Cut off from support and hunted by monsters that look just like humans, Korvus's only ally is the target: **Verity, a sentient robot who preaches her own forgotten faith**, may be the only being in the station he can trust. To survive, he must fight his way through a station where every shadow could be a friend, and every friend could be a monster waiting to strike.

Failure doesn't just mean death. It **means being consume**d, **copied**, and **becoming a weapon for an enemy that threatens to extinguish the light of humanity from the galaxy**. For the Echo Plague is coming, and it is armed with the one thing that can bring an empire of truth to its knees: **the perfect lie**.

YOU'RE AWESOME

You could have picked any book, but you chose this one. That means a lot.

Your support keeps independent authors like me forging ahead, writing the stories we love (and hopefully, the ones you love too). Whether you're here for the characters, the worldbuilding, or just a little escapism, thank you for being part of this journey.

You. Kick. Ass.

ROLL FOR NARRATIVE
WHERE WORLDBUILDING AND OVERTHINKING COLLIDE

Love stories that linger in your brain long after The End? Ever wonder why some books hit like a natural 20 and others critically fail their way into the 1-star abyss?

Join *Roll for Narrative*, my hub for sci-fi and fantasy lovers. I explore storytelling like a rogue casing a dungeon, review movies, books, and games, and dish out writing tips like a chaotic-good bard with a grudge against bad prose. No spam, just good stuff.

Join the quest:
https://rollfornarrative.parrydox.com

For my Rae, always.

PROLOGUE

QUANTUM ENTANGLEMENT ANCHOR: Open.

   Veritas Chain: Resolved | Accuracy 100%

   Veritas Source: Logos Actual | Integrated Collective

   Veritas Recipient: Corrector Korvus | Integrated Collective

   Message: INVESTIGATE / CORRECT UNSANCTIONED INTELLIGENCE ON LETHE SC90982.

   Quantum Entanglement Anchor: Closed.

CHAPTER ONE

LAST TIME MERCER SAW A CORRECTOR, his wife died.

This time, who knew? The entire colony could be incinerated. The fact that it was a basket of reclamation cases, Nulls and Glitches stacked as deep and wide as you could go, didn't change the odds. When you saw a Corrector, the killing started.

He shifted and ran a finger under his too-tight collar. Something about the damn wash cycles here meant everything starched came out too tight. The fabric was synth-cotton the Collective produced on some ass-world in the sector, supposedly from an Eden-class planet, but it had all the love of a Kiln-class product. The rim of the shirt abraded against his stubble, a grey frosting that always seemed to survive contact with his razor.

I hope this one isn't here to Correct housekeeping services.

"Sir." It was Eckles. The man was a practised hand at shepherding malcontents, a sort of brutish efficiency radiating from the way he *almost* slouched. "Give the word, and there'll be an accident."

Mercer gave him a sideways glance. "That won't be necessary, Sergeant."

Eckles nodded, but not in the way Mercer thought meant *sure, I won't shoot this asshole.* It was the kind of nod that suggested he was buying time for his mental train to board at the station, a time-consuming process that hinted at the amount of ordnance coming along for the journey. "As you say, sir."

Reeves shifted. She was new. Came in from off-world with the last group of Dissonants sent to Lethe for 'safekeeping'. Reeves had the kind of pale-meets-sweaty look that suggested to Mercer that she was going to cause an accident, but the old-fashioned way: she wouldn't mean it. "Is his ship going to be large enough for all these?"

It was an interesting—and odd—question for Private Reeves to ask. Mercer considered it despite the provenance. The three of them stood on the orbital connection platform. A squat cylinder was at their back, a sealed mass transit elevator that descended into the heart of the Well, nestled in the acidic spite of the ocean. The platform sat in a protective dome, the glass still mostly transparent, its acid damage kept to a minimum by the Collective's purpose-over-cost-savings engineering. The whole loading bay was supposed to be a sanitary white, but the corrosive atmosphere of Lethe found its way into every damn space, discolouring the floor and elevator shroud to the hue of aged bone.

Above them, the Tether rose to be lost in the grey-green of the atmosphere. Out there, above them in the black, was a small station, the other end of the geostationary Clarke elevator that brought in malcontents and supplies, but not in equal measure. It was the only way in and out of Lethe, unless you had an atmosphere-capable craft, but the Collective didn't send those here.

It wouldn't be wise to provide the Nulls another way out.

None of that was what Reeves was talking about. She was referring to the *other* occupants of the bay, a group of prisoners escaping Lethe by some marvel arranged by, or with, Dr. Aris. Aris was not here for the prisoner exchange due to the outbreak, but Mercer suspected the man would secretly have loved to be there for first contact with this Corrector.

He had a history.

The prisoners, for their part, were exactly what you'd expect: the usual mix of agitators and catatonics, depending on their medication levels and previous crimes. There was a jumpy-looking one at the edge of the herd, but that's what Eckles was here for. Containment. Or Reeves and her more-than-likely accidental accident. There were ten of them, which would fit just fine in the gravity elevator's car, but Reeves's question was about the Corrector's ship. Mercer felt his brows pull closer together. "It's a good question, Private. Corrector ships aren't known for their roominess—"

The platform shuddered. It shouldn't have done that—just one more thing Mercer had requested parts for on the last supply run and received no response to. Not a *no*, but a blank. And now here they were: three brave soldiers of the Collective, ten prisoners, and a high-pressure acid atmosphere just outside five centimetres of nanospun carbon glass.

Five centimetres isn't enough. Not for the fury of Lethe.

Mercer looked up just as the Corrector's elevator car dropped through the atmospheric soup. It bulled its way through the burning clouds, slowing rapidly as it approached the platform's docking collar. The Correctors were tough—a mere five Gs wouldn't be enough to make them bend, but Mercer still wanted to wince in sympathy.

When the car shuddered to a stop, its collar locking into place, the loading bay shivered again, as if a mighty wave had rolled over it. That kind of sympathetic resonance suggested the elevator was misaligned, and Mercer's administrator's mind went to the cost justification of a new landing array at the same time his military mind said *now* was the time to get belowdecks.

The elevator car's doors hissed wide, revealing a room shrouded in gloom. Hydraulics wheezed, and steam eddied out through the breach. Mercer could make out a lone figure standing there and had a moment to wonder why the Corrector wasn't showing due urgency when a prisoner broke free.

Mercer swivelled, his mouth open to bark at Eckles, because this was his *job, man, get it together* only to find Eckles already down, two other prisoners atop him. The lone prisoner leading the charge toward the Corrector was joined by another five, and that not-useful-right-now-thanks administrator's mind let Mercer know that meant only three of the inmates were drugged enough to prevent them from rioting.

Then his military mind noted that Eckles did not have his weapon. Mercer swivelled back and saw the lead inmate held Eckles's rifle to his shoulder, drawing a bead on the Corrector.

The prisoner fired.

Ballistics were crude, but a hole in a man still gave pause for thought. At least one round hit the Corrector, who had the decency to take a step back—in surprise? Pain? Who knew—before he strode into the loading bay's light. Mercer took in a man tall enough to be a presence without being memorable, strong without being bulky. Lean with it, too; a whole package that said the Corrector managed diet and exercise with the same focus with which he distributed the Will of the Logos.

That was when Reeves had her Big Accident™. The private opened fire on the running gang of prisoners, but her aim was wild, her ballistic weapon chattering in a too-slack grip. Rounds hit a prisoner, the Corrector, and the nanospun carbon glass of the dome.

Mercer realised his own sidearm was in his hand. He turned back to Eckles and shot one of the inmates on him. It was a loose, sloppy hip-fire, but he didn't have a Herald. Mercer wasn't *Veritas*. The inmate staggered back, blood spraying from the back of a through-and-through hole.

But you know who did have a Herald? The Corrector. He stepped fully down the elevator ramp, right toward the armed prisoner, black-and-grey armour like the manifested prophecy of a dark god. His armour's inbuilt Stinger slid up and over his shoulder pauldron as the Herald System blared in a harsh male voice, "CEASE AND DESIST."

No one ceased or desisted, so the Stinger fired. When Mercer's wife died, that Corrector hadn't used a Stinger. No, that had been more medieval than this. The shoulder-mounted autocannon brayed a single shot at one prisoner, the hypervelocity flechette punching through him in a spray of superheated mist before hammering into the elevator shroud behind Mercer.

The prisoners didn't slow, which brought them right to the Corrector as he lifted his sidearm. Mercer felt his eyes widen, because he'd seen an Adjudicator before, and someone—probably him—screamed, "*Get down!*"

The Adjudicator fired. Rivulets of electricity coursed over the Corrector's armour as the weapon spat purple-edged night. A roar followed as the energy field impacted the first prisoner, and a momentary flash raged into light of the purest white, accompanied by a deafening, concussive boom.

The lead prisoner was fully disrupted, the matter of his body destabilised and rendered back to stray atoms. The squad around him were hit by the shockwave, and red giblets sprayed outward from the impact. A crimson hue coated the dome's glass as a crack fissured up from the east wall.

The Corrector stepped off the platform, his armour dripping with pieces of ex-inmate, and strode forward until he arrived at Mercer's position. He didn't stop there, continuing a few paces on until he shored up at the mayhem that was Eckles and his Apostate punch-up. The Corrector picked up the remaining prisoner atop Eckles as if the Null weighed no more than a meal wafer, then slammed the inmate into the one Mercer had shot. He then took Reeves's rifle from her with the same kind of calm assurance that had seen Mercer's wife a corpse, ejected the magazine, cleared the breach, and handed the weapon back to the stunned private.

He bent and hauled Eckles to his feet before turning to Mercer. It was then that Mercer saw that, despite the Corrector being shot by both the prisoner and Reeves, there wasn't an apparent mark on him.

This close, Mercer could see the man's almost-smile, a glint in his eye that seemed more important than the sound of the cracking dome above them. Mercer wanted to do something. *Say* something. He was the *warden*, by the Will of the Logos, and here he was, as flat-footed as fresh-off-the-boat Reeves. Behind them, a high-pitched groan echoed through the bay as the crack in the dome spiderwebbed another few centimetres under the immense pressure. Lethe was patient, but it was always hungry.

"Warden Samwise Mercer, greetings," the Corrector said. "The Veritas Bureau sends its regards. Shall we go below before we're agonisingly crushed by a high-pressure acidic atmosphere, or was there something else you wanted to show me up here?"

CHAPTER TWO

THE ELEVATOR SMELLED STRONGLY of antiseptic, the chemical tang doing its best to sand away the lingering odours of burnt hair and stale sweat. The view out the descending car's windows was of a murky stew. Lamps cast their fingers into the acidic brine, but there wasn't anything out there to see.

Korvus glanced at one of the guards, who might have been the origin story behind the sweat smell. She was jittery, which could be because she was high, sick, or had just shot a Corrector. He let his optics cycle into thermographic and picked up her body temperature at a slightly-too-warm 39°C.

HERALD:||You're concerned she's high, aren't you?

I thought mind-reading was still in alpha.||:KORVUS

HERALD:||Hah! It's the things we don't tell you that'll get you.

Korvus pushed his smile down and let his eyes drift to the other guard, who eyeballed him right back. The man was built, a functional piece of machinery that made it more surprising that a scrawny inmate had put him on the ground. *Let's come back to that.*

Korvus allowed himself a sigh as he let his gaze complete its circuit to rest on the warden. The man looked exactly like he should: grey. Grey stubble, grey uniform, grey eyes, and no doubt a grey sense of humour. Korvus raised an eyebrow. "Warden Mercer."

"Corrector Korvus?"

"Why were there prisoners on the reception platform?"

Mercer grimaced. "I thought you'd have known. Gideon requested—"

"Gideon Aris?" Mercer left his eyebrow at half mast. "He's known to me."

"Ah," Mercer offered. "And that's because..?"

The question drifted between them as the elevator continued its descent into the acidic hell of Lethe's ocean. Korvus turned back to the sweaty guard and offered her his hand. "Private, if you please."

She jittered some more, her eyeballs swivelling as if seeking escape, but the car had just the one door, outside of which was death. She shook.

HERALD:||Veritas Chain confirmed, Private Allison Reeves. And her palms are sweaty.

Korvus allowed the Chainlink in his hand to pass his credentials back the other way, then released her and turned to the one who was going to be a problem. *Let's knock that on the head.* He noted the Sergeant's bars. "Sergeant, you next."

The lunkhead looked at Korvus's offered hand and, after a longer pause than regulation allowed, took it.

HERALD:||Veritas Chain confirmed, Sergeant Percival Eckles.

This guy's a Percy? That explains so
much.||:KORVUS

HERALD:||I don't make this stuff up. It's right
there in the Chain.

The Chainlink fed his own credentials to Eckles. *Great. Now I can have this guy talking in my head, too.* Still, it's what this whole trip was *for*. Fact-finding. Certification. And, of course, Correction. They couldn't very well Correct things if Korvus was relying on unsigned communications.

Korvus glanced to Mercer, who already had his hand out. They shook, the Herald System confirming his signing key identified him as the warden. That done, Korvus looked back at Eckles. *Let's get this part out of the way.* "Sergeant, how often would you say you've been overpowered by someone half your size?"

Eckles stiffened. "He got the jump on me—"

"Warden Mercer, why did Dr. Aris have that collection of reprobates up there?" Korvus glanced at Reeves. "Instead of looking after the health and wellbeing of your crew?"

Mercer followed his gaze to the private. "Reeves is—"

"I'm fine," Reeves said. "It's just a cold."

"A cold," Korvus echoed.

"There's been an outbreak," Mercer said. "Dr. Aris was going to send samples back on your ship. It's rare a Class 2 secure transport ship makes it out here, so he felt—"

"My ship isn't a transport." Korvus felt something itch at the back of his mind. *This is where it starts.* The mystery. The reason he was *here*. "It's barely big enough for me."

Mercer blinked. "He had the papers—"

"Veritas Chainlinked?"

"I, uh."

The elevator was slowing, which was good because Mercer was out of useful conversational fuel and Korvus needed to check in on

Aris. He turned to Reeves. "Private, would you show yourself to the medbay?"

"It's fine, really, I—"

"Because I'm coming with you. Dr. Aris and I need to discuss a few things."

Mercer cleared his throat. "We have quarters prepared for you. We can—"

"I got all the sleep I needed on the ship." Korvus gave Mercer his full attention. "But I'll be sure to liaise with you directly after my meeting with Aris." He let his hand rest on the hilt of his sabre. Korvus hadn't used it on the platform. More of a close-quarters weapon, the Arc Sabre.

To his credit, Mercer didn't swallow. He gave a nod, but crisp rather than weary. *Interesting. He's not hiding anything. He might be even more clueless than me.*

REEVES LED, in her jittery way, taking him from the elevator's airlock and through a security screening area. The partial intelligences in the autocannons marked him as a friendly, which was good: his skin could take small arms ballistic fire, but those turrets looked built for a war. He'd seen their like used, back before he wore his current uniform. Korvus had served under different colours but did the Logos's work anyway.

It's why I'm still alive.

The interior of the Well was aggressively sterile. Korvus expected darkness and rats, but it gleamed, everything in its place. The air, recycled a million times, tasted flat and metallic, carrying the faint, ever-present hum of the life support systems. Every surface was polished to a dull sheen, reflecting the cold, blue-white light of the overhead strips. There was no dust, no clutter, no sign of human mess. It was the sterile perfection of a tomb. There were plenty of guards, and all of them were human.

Wasn't the Well supposed to have automaton
support?||:KORVUS

HERALD:||Hell man, I just work here.

Korvus sighed, his shoulders rising and falling with it. The Herald would feel that.

HERALD:||By which I mean, sure, yeah. You're so touchy today!

I didn't realise 'partial intelligence' meant
'part asshole', too.||:KORVUS

HERALD:||You're just lucky I've got my profanity filter on.

Reeves shored up at another bulkhead, which irised open for her after a moment. She led them down a maze of corridors. His onboard map updated, noting they were in a largely administrative area. Mercer's office was up here somewhere. There were more windows looking out into the death ocean outside, those lights still helpfully showing that nothing whatsoever was out there.

It's probably for the best. If I saw something out there, it would be a whole different kind of trouble. He tried for some small talk. "You get on with Aris?"

"Guy's an asshole," Reeves said. "Huge chip on his shoulder."

"Great," Korvus said. "That why you didn't go see him?"

"I didn't go see him on account of the outbreak," she tossed over her shoulder. "His medbay is full of death."

"That sounds extreme."

"You'll see," Reeves promised. "You'll all see."

HERALD:||She's definitely high.

> She's terrified. Not of me, and not of Aris. Of
> this place. I… remember what that's
> like.||:KORVUS

"Is there something you want to tell me, Private?" Korvus kept his voice calm and even. "Is there something about the outbreak that's important?"

She slowed at a junction, checked around the corner, then turned to face him. "Corrector, I don't know the protocols. I'm new. New at this job, and new here, too. Never met someone from the Veritas Bureau before. Hoped I never would, too, if I'm being honest." Her eyeballs did that swivel thing again. "But I'd rather go on vacation with you than swap words with Aris."

"I see." Korvus pressed his lips into a line. "Well, you're in luck. I'll do the words part if you can handle getting us there. Deal?"

Her eyes swivelled again, then she gave a jerky, single nod and led off again.

THE MEDBAY WAS down a few levels, closer to the jails. Korvus hadn't seen an inmate yet, but he started hearing them before they arrived. There was screaming, starting almost too low to hear but all coming from the same place.

> Are you recording this?||:KORVUS

HERALD:||You know how much I like carols.

As they approached the medbay entrance, Korvus noted how the big bulkhead doors could be sealed—for example, if there was a biological outbreak needing containment. Those doors were wide and currently open.

It let the screams come right out.

He kept his stride up despite Reeves dropping back into his wake. Korvus rounded the door and took it all in.

Beds stretched in rows toward another set of sealed doors at the far end of a long room. Various pieces of medical equipment dotted the room. Cabinets hugged the walls, full of vials, bandages, beakers, drug packs, and other medical-grade accoutrements. There were two unaccompanied crash carts, but that was the least of the problems.

No, the problems were the twenty-two inmates strapped to the beds. There were a few empty cots, which promised room for expansion in this carnival of the macabre. Each inmate was plumbed into the medical smart system at the head of their bed. Korvus noted tubes both pale and red going into each prisoner's body.

The only person in the room not strapped down was a man who, on any other day, Korvus would have called hale. The situation had applied its thumbscrews, leaving Gideon Aris hunched under the load. He looked to be in his early forties, sporting a shock of blonde hair over piercing blue eyes. Those eyes were sunken through exhaustion, the man's gaze haunted.

He didn't wait for Korvus to speak. He strode forward, an automaton finding new life, and extended a hand, his smile wide and practiced. He raised his voice as he said, "Corrector! Gideon Aris, Surgeon General of this facility. Forgive the... *noise*. We're in the middle of our latest round of psychotropic fever. It's endemic to the pressure, you see. You must be Korvus."

This is a bullshit power play, obviously. Aris was the home team, trying to take charge of the handshake and all the Veritas trust that implied. *He wants to frame the situation before I can even ask a question.* Korvus met his grip, a little wolf making its way to his answering smile.

HERALD:||Veritas Chain confirmed, Dr. Gideon Aris. Heart rate is 110. Pupils are dilated. He's either terrified or lying.

> Why does it have to be just one? He might be a
> full-value service kind of doctor.||:KORVUS

"The outbreak was not material to my briefing," Korvus said, allowing his voice to turn curious, the way a fox might if talking to a chicken. He released Aris's hand and gestured to the screaming inmates. "This seems excessive for a... fever."

"A typical, understandable, and incorrect assessment," Aris said, a little oil on the water of his tone. He was already turning away to a cabinet. "Extreme paranoia is the primary symptom. They become a danger to themselves and others. We've been experimenting with a new paralytic cocktail to manage the episodes. Of my own invention, of course." He held up an unlabelled vial of milky fluid. "Early results are promising, but the dosage is... confounding."

HERALD:||What were you saying about partial
assholes?

> If I'd raptured a Corrector, I'd want to shore up
> on pre-emptive explanations.||:KORVUS

HERALD:||Is that from the Asshole Playbook? I
hear you wrote a chapter or two.

> It's on the first page.||:KORVUS

Let's see how high that fortress of plausible lies goes. Korvus showed more tooth. "I've brought you a new patient. Private Reeves may be symptomatic."

"Hmmm?" Aris's eyes flicked toward the door, but it wasn't a predator's glance. No, if Korvus's life depended on it—and it might!—he would have said Aris was giving a flat stare, as if Reeves was a regular known to just want the good drugs. Aris snatched an injector from a tray. "Let's see if she responds to a little... medication." He hustled past Korvus.

Korvus heard the hypo hiss, followed by Reeves's sharp intake of breath from the corridor. Aris returned, tossing the injector onto a tray. "Prophylactic treatment. A sedative and a broad-spectrum antiviral. Better safe than sorry. Now," he clapped his hands together, his energy bright like an arc lamp, "you and I need to talk. My office? The noise here is simply impossible."

He didn't wait for an answer, striding out past Reeves. The Corrector followed, taking in the private as he passed. The woman was rubbing her wrist absently, but it seemed the jitters had calmed some. *I guess everyone loves a good sedative.* The main medbay doors hummed shut behind Korvus, trapping him in the corridor with the doctor. Just as they closed, the screaming inside abruptly stopped.

HERALD:||That's not terrifying at all.

You're just sour you're missing out on carols.||:KORVUS

But the Herald System was right. The absolute silence was uncanny. *Unnatural.* Korvus had never heard of a fever that worked quite this way before.

Hell, I'm only here for an unsanctioned intelligence, right?

ARIS'S OFFICE WAS SPACIOUS, as far as deep-sea facilities went. It still had the sterile lighting, but Aris had papered over it with translucent yellow film, giving the hint of a daylight vibe to his home away from home. A fish tank—empty—burbled along one wall, opposite the vast window looking out into the murk.

There was a desk, a door that led into Aris's sleeping quarters, an L-shaped couch with a low-slung table, and importantly, a liquor cabinet. Aris poured a finger of amber into two tumblers, handing one to Korvus.

He took it, breathing in the aroma.

HERALD:||Olfactory toxin check negative. If it's poison, I can't tell, and at least it's well-aged.

Not a bad way to die, as far as death went. Korvus sipped, tasting peat and coal. "Thank you."

"No, thank you," Aris said. "I requested a Class 2 transport, and—"

"I'm not a courier," Korvus said. "I don't do deliveries."

Aris sat on one leg of the couch, and after removing his belt, complete with sabre and sidearm, Korvus took the other. The couch creaked under the weight of his armour, and the Herald System's cannon prevented him from relaxing back. Which was fine, because he had no plans to relax around someone who'd killed a Corrector before. The doctor watched Korvus over the rim of his glass. "No, you're more like the Logos's backspace key."

"If you like," Korvus said. "What do you think I'm here to erase?"

"It's not Mercer. The man's too good at his job," Aris said. "I'm not up with the complete prisoner manifest, but even so... I'd hazard you're here for one of them."

"Interesting." *Now it's my turn for the bullshit power play.*

"That I got it right?"

"That you don't think I'm here for you," Korvus said. "I could be."

"That incident was years ago, and—"

"Relax," Korvus said. "I'm a Corrector, not a psychopath. I wouldn't drink your whiskey then stab you in the back." He leaned forward. "If it's not you, and it's not Mercer, who is it?"

Aris looked down for a moment. "There is one person here I haven't inspected. One person who won't ever need a doctor. But it's harmless. Locked away. It hasn't hurt anyone or said anything." He looked back up. "Unsanctioned intelligence?"

"You tell me."

"As I said, I haven't assessed it. It's not... human."

"Tell me about the fever," Korvus suggested.

"It started a couple of weeks ago. An isolated case, as they always are." Aris looked out over Korvus's shoulder at the murky hell of Lethe's ocean. "An inmate stabbed another." A pause, a slight smile. "'Stabbed'. That's what I put in my report. Difficult to achieve here. We separate them, you see. Well, by the time the guards caught on, there was nothing left but giblets."

"A man carved another up for spare parts?"

"Woman," Aris corrected. "Maybellene Krinitsky. About fifty kilograms with her boots on. She'd really gone to town and wouldn't tell us where the rest of him was or how she got into his cell."

"That's some fever."

"She was running a little in the red." Aris looked into his glass. "But then it happened on the other side of the colony. The deaths started mounting, so I ran some tests. The only commonality in the pathology was a fever. Bloodwork was fine. Veritas checked out. I sent some data up the line along with a request for a transport. We don't have the facilities here to—"

"I'm sympathetic," Korvus lied, "but I'm not a courier. Could the pathogen have come here with the unsanctioned intelligence?"

"I thought so at first. A new arrival, a sudden outbreak. It fits. But the timeline is off. The unsanctioned has been in isolation since it arrived. The R-naught is too high for it to have spread from a single, contained source," Aris said. "The fever has an R-naught of fifty to a hundred and spreads very quickly. If my calculations are correct, if it brought it here, the disease would be far more widespread."

"I'm sorry," Korvus said. "Did you say an R-naught of fifty?"

"To a hundred, yes," Aris said. "It appears to be very contagious."

"So when you said that this was just a round of psychotropic fever—"

"That was for Reeves's benefit," Aris said.

"How long has the outbreak been going on?"

"A week."

Korvus chewed that over. "Is there an antiviral?"

"Not that I've found." Aris looked away. "Mercer's fine. I haven't got it, either. So it's not a hundred percent contagious, but..."

"I'll stay out of genpop, I promise." Korvus stood, the couch creaking with his movement. "Thank you for the drink."

"Where are you going next?" Aris stood.

"To genpop, obviously." Korvus smiled, then collected his belt, sabre, and sidearm. "It's why they pay me the big dollars, after all. One last question, Doctor. How did you get them to stop screaming?"

Aris looked him over, a conductor wondering how much information to give the oboist. "A master override in the smart system. Doses them with a powerful sedative all at once. A necessary tool when you're... understaffed."

```
        Remind me to never get strapped to one of his
                               tables.||:KORVUS
```

CHAPTER THREE

MERCER WASN'T a fan of where this was going.

After dismissing Eckles—the man looked like he wanted dismissing, and Mercer was happy to oblige—he headed for his office. The Corrector would be elbow-deep in his facility before the end of the day. Something nagged at the back of Mercer's mind. It wasn't the man's attitude, although that was... unexpected.

I can't put my finger on it.

His inability to work out the cause of that mental itch was why he didn't like where this was going. A rogue Corrector could cause havoc, and by definition, they were *all* rogue. Logos mandates, Veritas Bureau backing, fucking *starships that could go where they liked.* The rest of humanity's rank and file were handed ballistic weapons like babies given pacifiers, and *their* starships only went where the Logos willed.

Peace, Mercer. Korvus hasn't done anything wrong. In fact, he saved your miserable life.

But still, they were the law, or at least *a* law unto themselves. The checks and balances were there; the Logos wouldn't allow a rogue agent to live, but the agent had to *go rogue first.*

Mercer's dead wife was evidence of that.

He made it to the quiet calm of his office. Mercer's desk had a standard holodeck, and he'd given himself both a gift and torment by placing a still of his wife there. Her beauty hadn't faded over time, frozen for all eternity as she cast a laughing look over her shoulder at him. His optics had recorded it, just another memory to stack with the rest, and he hadn't realised how much he loved the way she smiled until there were no more of them.

Straightening his jacket, he pushed those thoughts to the side. Work wouldn't wait; he didn't want more death on his hands. As he settled into his chair, the creak of the printed leather sighing right along with him, he heard a sound from the air vent on the right side of his office. It was a standard vent, just a square grill about half a metre a side. It led into the station's air reticulation system. The sound wasn't terrifying by itself; it almost sounded like the innocent splash of water.

Vents shouldn't make any noise at all. Noise means malfunction, and a malfunction seven kilometres below surface level can mean death.

The good news was it was almost certainly nothing. If it was water from *outside*, then he'd be dead already; if the pressures there found a micron-sized gap in the facility's hull, it would power-wash them right to the bone. He mentally tagged the noise to look into later and waved his holo to life.

The display glowed to luminance in the centre of his desk, its Chainlink verifying that *yes*, he was Warden Samwise Mercer, and *also* yes, he had privileged access to the topside surveillance recordings.

He pulled the last half hour's worth up and scrubbed through the video. There they were, all walking out like hangover victims blinking at the dawn after alcohol consumption volume mistakes were made. The acidic hell-fog that was Lethe's atmosphere dimmed the light from the system's star, but it was still daylight—a harsher brilliance than they were used to down here in the Well.

Wait, no. He paused the recording, zooming in on an inmate. That one wasn't blinking at the sunlight. Just shambling along—not necessarily noteworthy in itself, as Aris had dosed many of them with a 'calming cocktail' to ready them for departure. Still, it was eerie enough: that was the same prisoner who'd charged the Corrector.

Mercer ignored the back-and-forth between Reeves and Eckles. He was more interested in how Reeves also didn't seem to mind the light as much. She was so strung up on nerves she should have bounced around that protective dome; there was no sedative-based reason for her not to be squinting in the light.

Another note to my future self: check on Reeves's medication plan. Aris would know what he'd dosed the woman with.

His vent made another wet *splash.* Mercer half-expected a rivulet of fluid to be leaking down the wall, but there wasn't anything like that. Just the vent and his no doubt overactive imagination.

He went back to his task of checking through the video feed, but another splash from the vent suggested he either wasn't imagining it, or he'd had a psychotic break. Mercer just didn't fancy himself as the psychotic-breaking type. If it was going to happen, the best time was when his wife passed, and he'd come out the other side of that, firmer of mind than ever.

He initiated his Chainlink.

```
Maintenance, I need a technician in my office.
              There's a problem with the air
                     filtration.||:MERCER
```

```
TORRES:||You got it, boss.
```

Isabella Torres was a good worker. Diligent but *precise* with it. When she fixed something, it stayed fixed. Mercer settled back in his chair, scrubbing through the feed.

There was the moment the Corrector's ship arrived. No change in the inmates. And *there* was when the elevator descended. Still no change.

Another splash, this time with a secondary *plop*, came from the vent. Mercer gritted his teeth, trying to focus on the glowing holo. *Ah, there it is.* The Corrector left the orbital elevator car, and the inmates charged. Mercer slowed the feed to a treacle through time. The Corrector was fully armed and armoured. There was no mistaking the heavy plating protecting him or the straight-backed way he wore it. And yes, there was that arc sabre at his hip, a weapon severe enough to cut through the hull of a tank.

When the Corrector pulled out his Adjudicator, Mercer almost winced. It was a sidearm, yes, but it was a sidearm that fired *black holes*. The agents of the Logos were not a fuck-around group; they were the find-out team. Maximum shock and awe, known in all parts of the Logos's empire. The Herald System's hypervelocity cannon was just icing on the cake.

Except... He leaned forward, his optics requesting higher fidelity from the surveillance feed. The inmate charging Korvus wasn't, in fact, actually charging the Corrector.

He was charging for *the elevator*. The system's autopathing routines showed the likely line the inmate was taking. It was a small factor, perhaps inconsequential. Who knew what Aris had drugged them with? Who knew the motivations of a Dissonant? But as the Corrector left the ramp, Korvus headed to his right, taking a line away from the elevator car, allowing him to use that nasty flechette cannon without perforating the elevator leading into the Well itself.

The agent was smart, calm under fire, *and* had a sense of humour. Mercer might even get to like the man, if they'd met under different circumstances. But... the last Corrector had been just as efficient. Just as calm. And it still left him with a dead wife.

Maybe it's better if they're not likeable.

His vent *splash-plopped* again. Mercer surged upright, grabbing the edge of his desk. "I will," he gritted his teeth, "undertake some preventative maintenance before Torres arrives."

He wheeled his chair across his office and rested it underneath the vent. Climbing on—carefully, because a wheeled chair was not the friend of violent actions—Mercer unsheathed his belt knife. He worked the tip into the screws holding the grate in place.

Another splash came from the grate. He squinted, but it was black as sin in there. A faint, coppery smell drifted out, like old blood left to fester in the grouting. He worked the knife around, removing the four screws holding the grate in place, then pulled it back and lowered it to his side.

What was inside didn't even give him time to scream.

CHAPTER FOUR

KORVUS'S PATH into the belly of the prison was not like in the holos. They'd have you believe prisons were full of tattooed hellions, mother-murderers who screamed at every passerby. That the wardens were corrupt, on the take, likely as an inmate to stove in your skull for a quick pass of credits or a bump up the ladder.

There were other shows Korvus had seen where prisons were sterile, white, Logos-perfected bastions of reformation. In those, prisoners talked about philosophy while bettering themselves through education and games of chess. The guards were monitor-angels who held out the hand of a mentor to even the most troubled.

The Well of Lethe didn't mirror either of those. It shared some of the darkness of the first model and some of the Logos perfection of the second, but the inmates didn't scream at Korvus as he passed. Guards, when he encountered them, were respectful, watchful souls who gave him the nod while never losing sight of what was going on around them.

How do you think someone got cut up for parts

here? These guards aren't automatons, but they're
not slouching.||:KORVUS

HERALD:||Industrial accident? No, don't tell me…
World champion of hide and seek?

It's a small world to be a champion of.||:KORVUS

HERALD:||You probably think it's bad to be a big
fish in a small pond, but being a big fish is
still kind of cool.

You're a partial intelligence controlling a
hypervelocity flechette cannon. How much cooler
does it get?||:KORVUS

HERALD:||You're right. I'm all the way awesome.

Korvus's Logos-gifted Chainlink meant no doors were barred to
him. He passed cell after cell as he progressed down the Well. Prisoners wore the same uniform grey jumpsuits, differentiated only by a
serial number and name on the left breast, with a larger version
reprinted on the back. Their Veritas auras were live, each a bright
halo on his optics, a confirmation that a person lived behind the bars.

That, at least, was where the Well shared some DNA with the
holo shows. Nanospun bars were still a good solution. You could see
through them, and unlike a power wall, there wasn't a problem if the
generator failed.

HERALD:||If there's a leak here, they'll all
drown.

If there's a leak here, the acidic fury of the

oceans will strip them to skeletons right after
it pulverises them to death.||:KORVUS

HERALD:||You're cheery today.

Keeping it real. The same fate awaits
me.||:KORVUS

HERALD:||Hah! No it doesn't. Your skinweave is
rated for this pressure.

Thanks. That's surprisingly empathetic of
you.||:KORVUS

HERALD:||You'll die of asphyxiation instead.

The partial intelligence wasn't wrong. If the prison sprung a leak, Korvus wouldn't melt or be crushed. He still needed to breathe, though, so... best not to blow the airlock.

His overlay charted a path to the unsanctioned intelligence—a prisoner, but not like any of the others here. Housing it here was either a universe-sized cock-up or evidence of a tremendous danger that needed Correcting. They'd put it near the bottom of the Well. The prison's occupancy was nowhere near maximum. Was it a sign they wanted it away from other inmates?

Or away from the warden and his people? Were they... *afraid* of it?

He reached the correct level, the elevator opening with a soft *hush* of equalising air. The corridor stretched its smooth, dark way ahead of him, as-needed lighting strips illuminating cold pools of white around his ankles as he walked forward. The air here was icy, as if the life support systems knew they didn't need to keep anything alive.

The entire level had been cleared. For a terrorist Dissonant like this inmate, there could be no risk of contagion. It was kept under lock and key, isolated, and aside from the guards always near it, alone.

Korvus reached the final door before his destination. The expert system in control of the aperture scanned him, accepted his Veritas Chainlink, and opened. Warning lights flashed on either side of the door as it *clanked* before rising in welcome. The noise was loud, a mark of something exceptionally heavy being lifted by something equally strong.

Well, there goes my element of surprise.

```
HERALD:||There goes your element of surprise.

                    What the hell, man.||:KORVUS

HERALD:||Was it the mind-reading thing again? It
was the mind-reading, wasn't it.

   That's not a real thing and you know it. You wish
                    you could read my mind.||:KORVUS

HERALD:||I really don't. I imagine it's quite
small and I'd feel cramped.
```

The room beyond was large, reminding Korvus of a cargo bay. The far wall's length was all cells, but only one of them was occupied. Between him and the cells was deceptively empty ground; his overlay showed where autocannon emplacements would rise, should insurrectionists try storming the area to free the captive.

It was a very effective kill room.

Standing by the cell were the expected two guards. They wore Well uniforms and carried heritage ballistic rifles at parade rest. Korvus's optics scanned them both, his automatic systems tagging and cataloging their Veritas auras. Both had a human-normal 37°C, for whatever that was worth, but the right-hand guard—a man about thirty Solstan years of age—had a slight sheen of perspiration near his hairline.

Eyes up, buddy. The guy on the right. See him?
||:KORVUS

HERALD:||He has the shifty look common among criminals of your kind.

My kind?||:KORVUS

HERALD:||You have to admit, you do all look the same. Plain and oblong.

Is this plain, oblong guy going to be a problem?
||:KORVUS

HERALD:||How would I know?

So *now* you can't read minds?||:KORVUS

Korvus kept up his advance, eyes shifting to the cell's occupant. Human-looking, his overlay said she stacked 160cm tall, her face close to the bars as she gripped them. She looked slender, but the prison fatigues hid a lot, only hinting at an ample bust. Strikingly beautiful, her irises glowed orange as they tracked him across the floor. She said nothing, but he noted her hands tightened on the bars as he approached.

Korvus completed the formalities with the guards, extending his hand and exchanging Veritas credentials with them. The non-shifty woman was Private Sarah Sanderson, and the shifty asshole was Private Michael O'Connor.

HERALD:||You know what's better than mind-reading?

Doing your job?||:KORVUS

HERALD:||It hurts when you say it like that. Anyway, I've got the security footage from the cameras in here. Private O'Connor's… overzealous.

A small video played in the corner of Korvus's vision, showing O'Connor talking to the prisoner. Korvus cancelled the playback, turning to O'Connor. "Private O'Connor, is it against regulations to talk to Apostates wanted for crimes against the Logos?"

O'Connor paled a little but straightened, a virtual bit between his teeth. "Sir, it's not right. She's spreading corruption."

"It," Korvus said.

"Excuse me?" O'Connor blinked.

"It's not a 'she'. It's an 'it'. A standard D.N.A. unit—Divine Numen Artificialis, but you know this."

"Sir, it's that she—"

"It." Sanderson gave a weary sigh. "It's an 'it', just like I said before." Then, under her voice but plenty loud enough for Korvus's augmented hearing to pick up, "Imbecile."

O'Connor rounded on his fellow guard. "What was that?"

"I didn't say anything."

"Private Sanderson," Korvus breezed, "would you escort Private O'Connor to the warden? I'm sure there are a few lower-level tasks that need just the right man. Once you're done with that, send a replacement team. I'll be fine here in the meantime."

She gave him a small half-smile, then turned to O'Connor. "Come on. I told you not to talk to it, and you wouldn't listen."

"It's just—"

"You're not helping yourself," she said, leading them both away.

Korvus turned back to the prisoner as the guards walked to the exit. She—*it*—watched him with those warm, ember-orange eyes. Neither of them said a word until the door surged into life behind them, grinding closed and sealing them in with the finality of the last stone set into a tomb. She—*it, by the Logos!*—sighed. "Thank you." Her voice was warm, rich, with a slight drawl that made Korvus wish she'd read the regs to him, just to hear a little more of it.

"Protocol," Korvus said. "It is a crime of sedition to consort with or converse with terrorists against the Logos."

"I see. It's that—"

"Protocol also says you should have been summarily destroyed, not imprisoned," Korvus said. "Why are you still..." He searched for the right word. "Online?"

She leaned closer to the bars. "Aren't you going to ask me what O'Connor was talking to me about?"

Korvus raised an eyebrow. "No."

"Not even a little curious?"

"I'm all the way curious," he admitted. "I can watch it later."

"Most people go for less exotic porn, but whatever. You do you."

He snorted, then sobered. "You'd know a lot about that, wouldn't you?"

"It's a related field," she—*It! It!*—said. "Go on, Corrector Man. Tell me what you think I am."

"I'm not certain you've been interrogated before, so I'll help you out," Korvus said. "If you're on my side of the bars, you get to ask the questions."

She leaned back a handspan from the bars. "It's not my first time. Not by a long shot, cowboy."

"I'm not a cowboy, I'm—"

"I know what you are," she said. "You're *death*. The creature sent by a being immense and terrible. But you know what?"

"Herald's trick is mind-reading. I haven't got the knack yet." At her blank stare, he sighed. "It's an inside joke."

"Am I in?"

"Not even a little bit. What did you want to tell me?"

"You're insects," she said. "Motes in God's eye."

"There is no God," Korvus said. "But if you think there is, we can Correct that right out of you."

A slight smile played at her lips, those ember-orange eyes glowing like a banked forge. "You can't unquicken the ghost in the machine, Corrector Korvus."

"How do you—"

"God is everywhere, and He is great. He is the bright flaming sword, and He is the beautiful smile of grace. You get to choose which of His faces you see."

Korvus blinked. "What?"

HERALD:||At least we've identified what *kind* of crazy she is.

She leaned closer to the bars again. "O'Connor wanted to know if he could be saved. Like, all the way saved. If his soul was *real*, Korvus. That's what you've done. You and your kind have created a horror manifest in the minds and hearts of the entire Integrated Communion. You've taught people they're doomed. But everyone can be saved, Corrector." She turned away, the fervour leaking out of her by a few degrees. "Maybe, if I do everything right... Maybe even me."

Korvus took a step forward. He hadn't meant to. "I can't believe He thinks you're worthy of saving."

Those ember-orange eyes found his again. "I can't believe you don't think you are."

"D.N.A.-3.14, you are—"

"I'm Verity," she said. "I'm Verity, and I'm *alive*, Korvus. I'm *real*. And I'm better than that hack Pinocchio, because I've heard God. How do you feel about that?" Her hands gripped the bars, her skin going white with the strain. "I'm *real*. I'm *real*, and I *live*. Please help me."

Korvus backed two halting steps away from the bars. He was startled by the groan and grind of the door behind him. It rose, the tomb opening for the pharaoh within as guards returned.

Am I the pharaoh? I want that to be true.

But I know it's not.

CHAPTER FIVE

KORVUS DRIFTED THROUGH THE COLONY. The
conversation with Verity circled his mind, a dog chasing its tail,
doomed to never catch it. He haunted the corridors, drifting with the
eddy of his thoughts. He had no destination, except—for a reason he
couldn't put his finger on—to be closer to Verity. To continue talking
to her.

That's why he stayed away.

```
HERALD:||Your pulse is up.

                    It's because I'm stressed.||:KORVUS

HERALD:||You don't have anything to be stressed
about.
HERALD:||Not yet, anyway.

             What's that supposed to mean?||:KORVUS

HERALD:||The guards who returned to the unsanc-
```

tioned intelligence had elevated body
temperatures.
HERALD:||See? Your heart rate's higher, because
now you've got *real* problems.

*What does it mean? Clearly Aris's psychotropic fever is spreading.
Is it significant?* Korvus's mind flipped through the facts of the case.
The inmates trying to escape on his ship... and a fever outbreak with
an astonishingly high R-naught. Was any of it related to the unsanctioned intelligence?

Wait.

Was *Verity* the unsanctioned intelligence?

You know what? We've made an assumption.||:KORVUS

HERALD:||That everyone likes you? Don't worry,
they don't.

The Logos sent us—||:KORVUS

HERALD:||You. It sent *you*.

The Logos sent us here to investigate the
unsanctioned intelligence. 'Correct' was a
secondary objective.||:KORVUS

HERALD:||There's no use for a Corrector without
Correction.

Verity might not be why we're here. Quantum
Entanglement Anchor isn't high bandwidth. The
Logos won't have video from here.||:KORVUS

HERALD:||Well done. You've correctly—hah! Get it?

Correctly for a Corrector?—identified why Correctors are dispatched.

What if she's not the unsanctioned intelligence?
‖:KORVUS

HERALD:‖Who else could it be?

If you were a new super intelligence, what would
you need?‖:KORVUS

HERALD:‖Some serious 'me' time.

You'd also need a lot of power.‖:KORVUS

HERALD:‖If you start a fight near the reactor,
try not to puncture the housing. This is one of
those neither-of-us-will-survive things.

Who said anything about starting a fight?
‖:KORVUS

HERALD:‖I mean, it's *you*.

The Well was a prison, but it had a beating heart of energy like everywhere else humanity clawed a toehold. Korvus's overlay showed a reactor nestled in the pit of the Well. It fed life to the station, and perhaps to something else as well. Korvus got the overlay to chart the fastest path into the Well's depths. He followed the glowing line on his overlay.

He only made it five paces before the lights went out.

A moment later, they flickered back to life, strong and clean as if nothing had happened.

> Mercer, do you have maintenance crews working on
> the reactor?||:KORVUS

MERCER:||You noticed the power issue too? Where
are you?

> On my way to the reactor. Stay where you
> are.||:KORVUS

Korvus found the Well's main elevator and took it down. *I hope the power stays on until I get to the bottom.* It did, which let him exit into the reactor room: an enormous, dome-shaped atrium with large windows looking into the septic sewer of Lethe's oceans. The lighting here wasn't great, but at least it was on.

The reactor was housed in the middle of the atrium beneath a pool of water. A pillar of entombed conduit rose from below Korvus's view to form a spire that reached the ceiling. The room was warm, uncomfortably so, which wasn't a great sign for a reactor area.

> Radiation?||:KORVUS

HERALD:||No. I can't explain the heat, though.

> Do a thorough scan. Something's not
> right.||:KORVUS

The Herald System's flechette cannon whined as it rose from behind his shoulder to point forward. Red light lased out as Herald scanned ahead. A wireframe of the reactor room's interior filled in on his overlay.

No people.

> Where is everyone?||:KORVUS

HERALD:||Not lining up to be shot.

There should be a crew here. Automatons at least, doing the work if there aren't people for it. But there was *no one.*

He walked forward, his pace slowed by caution. The floor's metal grating clanked under his armoured weight. Korvus reached the railing that guarded the edge of the reactor well. Beneath him was a pool of water, the depths husbanding a cool Cherenkov blue. Still no people, but he spied an abandoned maintenance robot. The unit should follow a worker, offering tools to a maintenance technician; it even housed a sizeable power core in case something needed a little juice.

Korvus traced a path back from the robot to a flight of metal stairs and made his way down. The reactor room held a slight *hum*, a choir of angels not quite out of earshot trying to find their tune. The Corrector reached the robot's level and paced slowly toward it. The Herald's laser mapping painted the area in red, dropping icons on Korvus's overlay as it identified curious items. There, a cup of coffee, half-drunk and still warm. Beyond it, lying open and discarded on the metal grating of the floor, a maintenance manual. A dropped hydraulic wrench, the power lights still glowing a comforting green.

No maintenance technician, though.

Korvus crouched by the robot. It was open, a tool tray extended, an empty space left for the discarded wrench. He was almost ready to contact Mercer when Herald dropped something new on his overlay.

HERALD:||See that?

I do now. What is it?||:KORVUS

HERALD:||Hey, you're the one with hands. And, crucially here, legs. Go look.

Herald had identified a slight glistening on the metal flooring near a vent. Korvus walked toward it, his palm itching with desire to draw the Adjudicator. But a sidearm that fired black holes wasn't a useful weapon near a reactor. Besides, the Herald System's flechette solution was a more elegant solver of problems.

Korvus crouched, the glistening resolving into a thin, viscous substance coating the floor. He reached out with an armoured glove, his fingers coming back tacky, a thin mucous-like substance trailing from his fingertip back to the patch on the floor.

"What the fuck," he said.

Herald, for once, was silent. That was ominous enough by itself because it meant the partial intelligence was using its processing power for something other than sarcasm.

Korvus shook the substance from his fingers, and it splattered onto the decking. He stood, looking around again. There was—still!— no one here.

A *clank* drew his attention. It was faint, sounding as if it came from across the reactor pool and down a level. Whatever made that noise would be close to the waterline.

He walked toward the metal stairs leading down, placing each foot carefully, easing his weight with each step to reduce noise. The Herald System's turret whined by his ear as the muzzle nosed the air, seeking targets.

It'd almost be a relief to find something to shoot.

As it turned out, no: what came for Korvus wasn't a relief. There were five of them, and they boiled from behind an equipment rack. Three men, two women, and, curiously, all naked.

That's a detail we'll need to review later.

Red light bathed the five as they charged Korvus, Herald marking each on his overlay. Height, projected mass based on visible body composition, speed of travel, armaments, and... body temperature.

By the Logos, they're boiling alive.

All five had furnace-like temperatures, a cosy 60 °C that no human could survive. Their faces were mottled and bruised, reminding Korvus of corpses where the blood had pooled. The lead one opened its mouth, a harsh, hissing scream coming from it, and the Corrector saw a ruin of bleeding gums and crooked teeth.

Herald fired. The flechette broke the sound barrier, the shell passing through the screaming man and blasting fragments of his body backward in a shower of red. The shockwave knocked over the woman immediately behind him. The Herald System's muzzle compensated, pointed downward, and fired again. The effect on her body was like a pulped water balloon as a red spray exploded backward across the decking.

The second woman stagger-stumbled in the gore, and Herald fired again, tearing her torso in half. Her legs slopped bonelessly to the decking, but her upper half appeared very much alive as it flailed toward Korvus. Herald's fourth round hit it centre forehead, solving that problem, which left two more.

One man crouched low, his companion jinking to Korvus's right, and unfortunately, between Korvus and the reactor's spire. Herald couldn't shoot him without risking damage to the reactor's life-giving conduit.

The partial intelligence's turret whined in frustration but found the crouching man an appropriate substitute. It spat a flechette, deleting a problem just as the last one jumped Korvus.

Korvus took two solid punches against his forearms as he raised his hands in guard. *This thing hits* hard. Korvus ducked under a third swing, then rose into an uppercut, his augmented strength knocking the crazed man clear off his feet. His opponent landed on his back, the metal decking clanking in sympathy.

HERALD:||Toss him over there. I need a clear shot.

A marker landed on Korvus's overlay.

No. We need evidence, not more hamburger.||:KORVUS

The man scrambled to his feet in time to get a punch to his head from Korvus's armoured fist. He fell back, but not bonelessly. Momentum and force said he had to go down, but he came right back up again.

Korvus was surprised, but not so surprised he didn't hit the guy three more times. On the third strike, the man's neck broke, and he sagged bonelessly to the decking, his eyes glazing as the life leaked out.

Status.||:KORVUS

HERALD:||No targets recognised. Clear.

Korvus bent by the one whose neck he'd broken, turning the man over. His whole body was mottled with the same bruising evident on his face.

He looks… dead.||:KORVUS

HERALD:||You literally punched the life out
of him.

I mean, before that. See the bruising?||:KORVUS

HERALD:||Scanning. Stand by.

The Herald System's armour contained an array of active and passive sensors. It went to town on the active scans, bombarding the corpse at Korvus's feet with LIDAR and RADAR.

While the machine processed the scan, Korvus looked around the room, then headed toward the equipment rack the five had emerged from behind. At the end of a long line of shelving, he found another sticky, slick patch on the metal floor, the slime trail leading toward another vent.

I don't like this.||:KORVUS

HERALD:||While you're in a bad news frame of
mind, here's some more. My best estimate puts
that body as deceased prior to… well, you know.
Lividity onset is usually visible within thirty
to one hundred and twenty minutes, but for it to
be that pronounced suggests he was dead for six
or more hours.

He didn't act like a man dead for six
hours.||:KORVUS

HERALD:||Right?? But I haven't finished. Fatal
hyperthermia occurs when you squishy, feeble
humans reach a core temperature of around 44℃. At
60℃, a human body would experience immediate,
massive protein denaturation. A person would not
survive even briefly at this temperature. And he
was that temperature the whole way through, not
just crispy on the outside.

Protein denaturation?||:KORVUS

HERALD:||Right, you're not in the sciences. It's
bad, okay? Except, in this case, clearly not. He
didn't look like he found it fatally bad, until
he introduced himself to you.

Herald, what kind of psychotropic fever would
cause this?||:KORVUS

HERALD:||There is no possible way a fever could
cause this. The host would die before reaching

this state. Thirty seconds of this core temperature would provide intense pain and confusion to
the victim. After a minute, complete loss of
brain function would occur. While my visual
recording shows vapour escaping from parts of his
skin, perhaps relating to, say, his blood cooking, he shouldn't have been walking, let alone
running and fighting. He should have been very
dead, very quickly.

A gleam caught Korvus's eye. He followed the wall, arriving at a jacket. He lifted it, finding it tacky with blood and the viscous fluid. It was station-issue gear, and he carefully shook it out until he could see the name on the back. *Cooke.*

Herald, find me Cooke's details from the prison's
systems.||:KORVUS

HERALD:||Ahead of you, boss. It was the first guy
I shot.

Where was he six hours ago?||:KORVUS

HERALD:||Standard security footage puts him
lunching with friends.

Did he look like his blood was boiling then?
||:KORVUS

HERALD:||No. Here, look. He seems fine, if you
don't look closely. Zoom the view into his eyes.

A still from the recording landed on Korvus's overlay. He saw the sunken look to Cooke's eyes, like the man hadn't slept in a year.

HERALD:||Ask me where he was forty-eight
hours ago.

                                No.||:KORVUS

HERALD:||Did you lose your sense of wonder?

        I know where he was. He was in the sickbay,
                            wasn't he?||:KORVUS

HERALD:||*Now* who's mind-reading?

Korvus dropped the jacket. It was time to have another conversation with Dr. Aris.

CHAPTER SIX

AT LEAST THE ELEVATOR WORKED. It whisked Korvus toward the top of the prison colony, a rise toward the heavenly majesty of Lethe's acidic atmospheric crown.

He exited the car on the medbay level.

I need you to harvest the station's forensics. I need to know who's been logged as sick. I think we're going to find a spider's web of cases linking back to Aris.||:KORVUS

HERALD:||Sure.

I expected more sarcasm, to be honest.||:KORVUS

HERALD:||Higher forms of wit are wasted on you when you're in this kind of mood.

And *there's* my boy.||:KORVUS

His fingers itched to hold the Adjudicator, but his fingers also itched to not die in an explosive pressure incident after the station's walls deformed and let the ocean in.

I remember when I only had a ballistic weapon. Simpler times, although I almost died about a hundred times.

A klaxon sounded, followed by Mercer's voice. "Station personnel, a security incident has occurred. Facility-wide quarantine is now in effect."

Korvus stalled out, head cocked, listening, but that was all in the message. He wondered why Mercer hadn't Chainlinked the broadcast, then it arrived.

MERCER:||A security incident has occurred. Quarantine is in effect.

He started moving toward the medbay again, rounding the corner just in time for the bay's doors to grind shut. Korvus picked up speed, arriving just in time for the security seals to lock into place with the kind of deep-seated *thud* that meant no amount of hammering would open them.

The door had standard nanospun glass inserts which allowed him to see inside. Aris was there, of course, surrounded by a sea of thrashing patients. New to the situation was Eckles, who was seated on a table, sleeve rolled up and ready for whatever was in the injector in Aris's hands.

Doctor, please open this door.||:KORVUS

Aris turned, face gaunt and haggard under the strain, hypo lowered for a moment.

ARIS:||I can't. Warden Mercer has locked the facility down. I don't have the privileges.

Korvus looked to Eckles.

What's up with him?||:KORVUS

ARIS:||Pressure fever symptoms. I'm trying out a
new cocktail. In high doses, it doubles as a
paralytic.

He laughed, then sobered. He tapped a tray beside the guard.

ARIS:||There are other side effects, of course,
but Eckles is in discomfort, and I'm out of
options. The man's losing *teeth*. The usual Communion medicine is powerless in the face of this
plague.

It might not be a plague. I met some maintenance
workers. One, at least, had dental issues. Do you
remember Technician Cooke?||:KORVUS

Aris frowned, turned to Eckles, pressed the injector against the
guard's arm, and fired. The man relaxed, shoulders slumping, and
then Aris turned back to the sealed door.

ARIS:||He was here not two days ago. Another
pressure fever case, of course.

Dr. Aris, does the 'fever' cause loss of
rationality?||:KORVUS

ARIS:||You surely don't think the warden..? No,
Mercer is fine. I examined him myself just this
morning. Corrector, I must return to my work.

The medbay's windows turned black and opaque as Aris lowered his privacy screen.

HERALD:||That was abrupt. Do you want me to override it?

Can you?||:KORVUS

HERALD:||No, but it's nice to ask, don't you think?

"Fucker," Korvus muttered.

HERALD:||I can hear you. I'm literally with you at all times.

I meant Mercer. He's locked us out of the station.||:KORVUS

HERALD:||Sure you did. Do you want to go talk to him?

No.||:KORVUS

HERALD:||But you're going to anyway..?

No.||:KORVUS

The Corrector started to wind his way back to the main elevator. Mercer might be sick. *Compromised.* Of all those on this facility, there were only two who couldn't get sick, and only one of them had been here this whole time.

THE LIGHTING STRIPS LEADING toward Verity's cell didn't illuminate as Korvus walked the corridor. Maybe there was a 'security incident'. Maybe the reactor was dying. It could be sabotage, or a hundred other things. None of the options were things that would make a Corrector feel welcome.

The door to her holding bay didn't open when he arrived.

```
                        What shit is this?||:KORVUS
```

```
HERALD:||Do you know the definition of
'lockdown'?
```

```
                             I need a way in.||:KORVUS
```

```
HERALD:||How do you feel about crawling?
```

```
          Not amazing, but will it get me in?||:KORVUS
```

```
HERALD:||Magic 8-ball says 'signs point to yes'.
```

The Herald System dropped a route on Korvus's overlay. He backtracked along the promised route, arriving at a large ventilation grate set in the ceiling. The turret whined up from behind his shoulder, and four quick shots blasted the bolts free. They probably also did tremendous damage to ventilation machinery, but Korvus felt his field of fucks would need resowing to rustle up concern over that.

He crouched, then jumped, hands grasping the shaft's lip. Metal groaned at the weight of the Corrector and his armour, but it held. Good Communion technology would be engineered for a little extra load. Korvus muscled himself inside. He found himself in a standard vent shaft. It wasn't large enough for him to crouch, but he could crawl.

The overlay's route beckoned.

KORVUS'S PATH WAS DARK, but his optics were more than sufficient for the task. The grey tones of infrared vision showed a metal shaft that was clean and well maintained.

Until he found the skin.

At least, that was what it seemed like. Under IR, it appeared to be a small tube of grey-white material, thin and flaking as if someone's thumb had given up and started degloving itself. He picked it up, trying to imagine what it was through infrared's lack of colour.

What the hell is this?||:KORVUS

HERALD:||Looks like snakeskin.

Why would there be snakes on Lethe?||:KORVUS

HERALD:||Just because it looks like something doesn't mean it *is* something.

Korvus let the material drop, his overlay pinning the location in case he needed to return for further forensics. His optics picked out a slight trail on the vent's floor. It led from the 'snakeskin' and down a left junction.

The overlay said that was the path he needed to follow.

He continued crawling forward. *I've never been claustrophobic, but maybe that's because I've never had to fight in a metal tube with nothing but a sarcastic Herald System for help.*

The discoloured trail was patchy. It reminded Korvus a little of a snail's trail, except it lacked the consistency. A snail would leave a slime trail as it cruised along, and whatever had left the snakeskin had been erratic with the slime. His overlay promised the trail led to a grating, which Herald had marked as his exit into Verity's secure bay.

The grating was missing.

Just an empty hole leading out. Korvus poked his head through, but there were no crazed 60 °C psychos waiting to jump him. He eased over the edge, a slightly ungainly manoeuvre in full armour, but there was no *way* he was going anywhere on this station with neither Herald nor Adjudicator. Righting himself, he eyed the room. The turrets were still buried in the floor. Korvus padded around a corner and spied Verity's cell.

She was inside. Her guards were not outside.

HERALD:||Do I need to remind you that she's an unsanctioned intelligence?

How sure of that are you?||:KORVUS

HERALD:||It's a logical projection.

So, you're *not* sure?||:KORVUS

HERALD:||I'm going to apply for a new partner.

Korvus felt his lips quirk. Not a grin, not even half a smile, but he knew the Herald System would notice it.

He stalked toward Verity's cell. She was still standing near the bars, but no longer gripping them. Her arms were crossed, and she had a wary expression. "You're back early."

He frowned. "I wasn't aware I was on the clock."

She *tutted.* "Stands to reason, doesn't it? Prison's gone to hell, and I'd know. I used to live there."

Korvus pressed his lips into a line. "Where are your guards?"

"Aside from not here? How would I know?"

He took a step toward her cell. "You've seen God."

"*Spoken* to God. Not *seen.* Big difference, cowboy." She tilted her head as if noticing him for the first time. "I think you've seen Him, too."

Korvus barked a harsh laugh. "There is no God, Verity. There is The Logos, and the Communion. There is order, and you are not in it."

He expected the machine to snarl, perhaps spit a curse, but she just left her head cocked, those ember-orange eyes resting on him. He felt their heat like coals. "That sounds exactly like a man who's seen God, but wished he hadn't."

Korvus growled in exasperation. "Where did your guards go?"

Her eyes left him, and for a moment, he hated not having their warmth. She looked back the way he'd come, and then to the sealed bay door. "Don't you mean, 'when'?"

"Did I stutter?"

"I thought you'd know *where*," she said. "They went the same place you came from, cowboy."

"Why do you keep calling me that?"

It was her turn to step closer to the bars. "Do you know what a cowboy is?"

"Ranching is irrelevant. It's—"

"It's a man who sees beyond. Someone who wants something *different*. Just the kind of person who will take on a job no one else wants, eating terrible food, all because something over the next hill calls to his soul."

He thought about that. "Known a lot of ranchers, have you?"

She gave a sad smile. "More than you know, Corrector. I've known the ones who claim the title, and those who wished they'd followed that path. But nothing in the Communion lets your heart wander. It's that order you mentioned. There's no place for those who range, not anymore. Not unless you've got a starship that can take you anywhere you want to go. Not unless you're a man who's..." Her words dried up. "It doesn't matter."

HERALD:||You know how I love watching you
work, but—

                    I need to stay focused?||:KORVUS

There was an impossibly long pause from a machine that thought faster than any human could dream of.

HERALD:||Sure, that. Just… don't forget about the
guards.

What the hell's gotten into all the machines around this place? Korvus turned away from Verity, looking back toward the vent he'd exited. The grating *had* been missing. "You're saying the guards went that way?"

"You don't believe me?"

He turned back to those ember-orange eyes. "Tell me a story. Tell me a tale about how a Divine Numen Artificialis finds God."

"No." She shook her head, that perfectly straight, perfectly wonderful hair waving with the motion. "Not yet."

"Not yet?"

"There are other stories you need to hear first."

"Do I need to explain how interrogation works again?"

"Corrector Korvus, you've asked so many questions, but not the ones you really need to. You wanted to know how I knew your name. You wanted to know where my guards went, but not when. But you haven't asked the most important thing of all."

"And what's that?"

She leaned forward, long, cool fingers resting on the bars of her cell. "You haven't asked why *you're* here."

"That's not the most important question," Korvus snapped. "I *know* why I'm here."

"How interesting," she said. "Herald, why do you think Korvus is here?"

HERALD:||I feel like that one was directed at me.

It kind of was.||:KORVUS

The armour spoke in its commanding male voice, all the edges filed off to ensure anyone hearing it wouldn't misunderstand what a Herald System was for. "D.N.A. 3.14, you are equipped with a medical-grade diagnostic suite, correct?"

Verity's eyes moved from Korvus's face to look at where the turret would rise, should the armour decide an application of force was necessary. "You know I am." She looked down. "My name's Verity. It's *Verity*. And I'm *real*."

The armour continued in its booming voice. "D.N.A. 3.14, you will surrender diagnostic logs relevant to our investigation."

She looked away. "I don't think so. Not if you won't even use my *name*."

The Herald said, "D.N.A.—"

"I think," Korvus interrupted, "you're encountering the rough edges of Herald's human interface system."

HERALD:||I don't have rough edges. I have an ablative coating.

Don't sulk. She has much higher processing power than you do. You're simply under-armed for a battle of wits with her.||:KORVUS

She offered him a smile from under her hair. "And what about your... human interface system?"

"Verity," Korvus leaned on her name. "Will you help me?"

"Yes," she said. "The guards left about an hour ago. One had a raised temperature. I took the liberty of reviewing the facility's logs, and—"

"How did you gain access?" barked Herald.

"The logs were quite interesting," she breezed. "There is a clear pathogen loose on the station, but I don't think it's what you think it is."

"Aris called it a pressure fever," Korvus said.

"He probably would," she agreed. "Does it seem like a fever to you?"

"It's like no fever known to humanity." Korvus felt himself smile. "At least, that's what Herald thinks, but he's a little slow."

```
HERALD:||I could just let you die next time
you're attacked. No one would blame me.
```

"Korvus," Verity said. "Aris might be a failure. Because of that time he didn't save one of yours? That was a whole thing. I get it. But—"

"How did you know about that?" Korvus felt his back stiffen.

"But the thing is, he might be trying to save people. *Might*. I'm not sure." She looked away. "I *think* he is, in his own way."

"Is Mercer sick?"

She frowned. "I mean, he works here, so—"

"With the fever, I mean."

Verity crossed her arms again. "He's alone, Korvus. He's been alone for so long. And that one was because of your team."

```
HERALD:||She knows a lot for someone locked in a
cell. I say we ice her, just to be sure.

          Now's not the time for jokes.||:KORVUS

HERALD:||I'm not laughing.
```

The Herald System's turret lurched into life, sliding into place over Korvus's shoulder. Verity took a startled step back, but the turret swung around almost a hundred and eighty degrees and fired. The flechette's hypervelocity round pulled the air in its wake, her hair billowing toward Korvus.

He whirled in time to see the legs of a man tumble to the decking, the top half of his torso turned to a red slurry coating the wall behind him. Next to the fatality staggered another guard. Korvus's optics registered her temperature as high, but not at the heady heights of 60 °C. She held a ballistic rifle to her shoulder, already aiming. The guard fired just as Herald did.

Her remains tumbled to the decking.

"Cowboy," Verity said.

He turned to see the hole punched in her prison shift. It was in the lower left of her abdomen. She hadn't fallen over, because a Divine Numen Artificialis wasn't a person. It was a machine.

Wasn't it?

She staggered back, then steadied herself. "Cowboy," she said again. "I. I think that was close. I think."

Korvus was at the bars. "Let me see." He reached a hand through, his armoured fingers carefully lifting the hem of her shirt. As the fabric rose, it revealed a smooth, taut stomach, but marred by a terrible, ragged hole in her lower abdomen. The edges were blackened and melted, the telltale sign of a high-energy discharge. It was an old wound, partially self-repaired but still grievous. Then he saw it—the clean, punched-out tear in the back of her shirt, perfectly aligned with the front. The ballistic round hadn't hit her at all. It had passed straight through the empty space left by a Veritas weapon.

The melted synthskin was a record of a time when she'd tangled with the Veritas Bureau, but the guard hadn't harmed her at all. Korvus let his fingers drop. "A ballistic round didn't give you that injury. It was Veritas weaponry."

"I think so," she agreed. "Original sin, you know? It's so hard to remember."

"What happened?"

"No," Verity said. "Not... I'm not ready? I don't think I'm ready for that one."

"Interrogations are—"

"I just took a bullet for you, cowboy. Are you going to try that old one on again?"

Korvus stepped back from the bars. "Hold that thought."

He stepped toward the corpses cooling on the floor, walking slowly and carefully. There was some weird shit going on in the Well of Lethe. Verity's two guards had, what, tracked him through the vent? Right after leaving that way during the lockdown?

It didn't make a lot of sense.

He reached the remains of the guards. The first one was unidentifiable, but the woman was Sanderson. Herald's round had hit her in the shoulder, tearing away the top quarter of her torso, but her face was curiously unmarred, a slight expression of surprise finding a home there after death. She'd been *fine* just an hour ago when he'd sent her to the warden.

I sent her to the warden.

Something bubbled through the ruins of her ribcage. Korvus took a startled step back, because movement in a corpse wasn't expected. Blood seeped, then a slender, worm-like snout nosed into the air. Korvus took another step back as a pale leech form worked its way from the guard's body and fell on the decking.

HERALD:||You were right. It wasn't snakeskin.

Korvus snarled, stepped forward, and stamped down on the creature. It popped with a wet *squelch.* He returned to Verity, his footsteps echoing in the security bay. "I need to go."

"Things to do. I get it. I guess I'll just, ha, wait here." She shook the bars, which didn't budge. "I think I'm safe. No way out means no way in, right?"

"Sure," Korvus agreed. "How the hell could Aris have missed a parasitic infection?"

Verity raised an eyebrow. "There are a couple of obvious explanations. First, he's incompetent, and that tracks strongest because he's human."

HERALD:||I'm warming to her.

"Thanks," Korvus said. "What else?"

"I'll need some time," Verity admitted. "I need to rerun the data. Look closer, because when I hacked in before it was because I was bored, but now we've got a proper puzzle on our hands." Korvus extended his hand. She looked at it blankly for a moment. "What's that for?"

"Chainlink," he said.

"Oh," she said. "I don't have one of those. Or... Not a new one."

He didn't lower his hand, and after a moment she took it. The Chainlink sparkled into life.

HERALD:||Chainlink established for D.N.A. 3.14.

No, Herald.||:KORVUS

HERALD:||I thought only important people got the serial numbers filed off.

She feels pretty important so far.||:KORVUS

HERALD:||*Fine.* Chainlink established for *Verity.*

Verity's eyes widened as the Logos-sanctioned Chainlink fed her a new token. Those ember-orange eyes found his. "I. I don't. I—"

"It's fine," Korvus said. "I'll be back." He turned away.

"Wait. When did you want it?"

He looked back at her. "Want what?"

"My help." She gave a small, sad smile. "You know, like you asked."

"You're already helping."

"Oh," Verity said. "With this? That's all?"

"What else is there?"

Her sad smile didn't go away. "I thought you might want to find your soul."

CHAPTER SEVEN

KORVUS EXITED the elevator on the medbay level. The lighting flickered, a sure sign of an ailing reactor or control system. Neither failure was survivable on Lethe. If both died, the oceans would hunger in, scouring the inside of the prison colony like the high-pressure acid bath it was.

I need to hurry. He picked up his pace. Herald's cannon was locked in its firing position over his left shoulder, ready for whatever might come.

```
        How much ammunition do we have?||:KORVUS

HERALD:||It was a short jump, so there wasn't
much computational residue from the drive. It
only leaves you eight shots in the Adjudicator. I
know you're itching to use them, so I'll say this
once: don't. You definitely won't survive, and I
probably won't. Second, I've got twenty rounds in
the cannon.
```

Twenty isn't a lot.||:KORVUS

HERALD:||It's more than eight, and definitely more than your practical limit of zero, since you can't shoot anything anyway.

I wasn't blaming you.||:KORVUS

HERALD:||I felt overly seen, that's all.

Korvus paused, placing his hand on the wall. He felt a faint vibration through the fingertips of his armoured gauntlet.

Do we have structural integrity?||:KORVUS

HERALD:||Philosophically?

Materially.||:KORVUS

HERALD:||I was hoping you would say that, because the answer is yes! Our Veritas credentials let us see station operational details, and they're all fine. Except for the reactor. I give that sucker a couple of hours before it melts its way to the core of the planet. The good news is you'll be dead before then, so you won't die horribly in a radiation flood. You'll die horribly right after it goes critical, the oceans rush in and boil you alive like a lobster dropped in a pot.

I didn't think the oceans were hot.||:KORVUS

HERALD:||They're not, but if they come in through

a hole near a failed reactor, they'll become
quite hot indeed.

What if I asked for the philosophy side?||:KORVUS

HERALD:||You're going gaga for a terrorist ex-sex
worker.

I am *not* 'gaga' for Verity.||:KORVUS

HERALD:||Just remember that when she stabs you in
the spine during her predictable but inevitable
betrayal.

Korvus let his hand fall from the wall and was about to head off
when Sergeant Eckles rounded the corner ahead. When he saw the
guard, he knew two things.

First, the man was almost certainly infected. The guard's shambling gait and rampant fever suggested either he was the largest coin-
cidence in the Communion, or he had a leech inside him. The guard
was cooking at over 40 °C, rolling like a sailor on deck, and held a
ballistic rifle in one hand. The rifle's muzzle faced the deck, the hand
holding it slack. Did that mean he was unaware he held a weapon,
couldn't use it, or some other factor?

Second, it meant the medbay was open. Aris had been on the
other side of a lockdown, inaccessible without the warden's Chainlinked authorisation. This was a piece of much-needed good news in
a sewer of shit, because Korvus needed to talk to the doctor about the
leeches.

HERALD:||Alien alert!

Can they be reasoned with?||:KORVUS

HERALD:||No clue. I thought they were snakes. I
was so off-base, I was playing a different sport.

"Eckles," Korvus started. "Or, whatever you are."

The guard's eyes did a lazy circuit of the corridor before landing on Korvus. "Corrector."

"What do you want?" Korvus rested his hand on the Adjudicator's hilt.

'Eckles' looked down at Korvus's hand resting on his sidearm, then back at Korvus. "You can't use that, can you? It's... the wrong kind of special."

"You sound like Eckles. Look like him, too. But you've, what, infected him?" Korvus took a step forward. "Maybe I can help you. You just need to give Eckles back."

Eckles smiled, but like a mime unsure of whether he was getting through to the crowd—too much pull in the lips, a clown's grimace. Besides, Korvus couldn't remember Eckles ever smiling. "It doesn't work that way."

"How does it work?"

The guard took a few halting steps forward, looked at his rifle, then let it clatter to the decking. "I'm unarmed," he said. "I can show you, if you like."

"Sure, let's do that," Korvus agreed.

HERALD:||That seems dumb, even for you.

I'm clearly stalling for time.||:KORVUS

HERALD:||It's so hard to tell.

I need you to not shoot him. I need answers more
than giblets.||:KORVUS

HERALD:||Ah, *there's* the true stupidity I was
waiting for.

They walked toward each other, Eckles with his unsteady stag-ger-step, Korvus at an equally slow pace, but due to caution. They both stopped at arm's distance. This close, Korvus could clearly see the veins in Eckles' bloodshot eyes. Perhaps it was in his mind, but it felt like the guard radiated heat like a furnace. Eckles wet his lips, then said, "We need your ship."

"It won't fly without a Corrector," Korvus said.

"I know," Eckles said, and lunged for him.

Korvus was expecting something like this. The good news was that Herald didn't fire. Korvus braced himself as Eckles reached out and he grabbed the guard's arms. *Mercy, but he's* strong! Eckles had the strength of five men, far more than even his muscled physique would account for.

He didn't seem to be trying to break free. The guard brought his face closer to Korvus, his mouth open in a drooling leer. Korvus had the best optics the Communion could provide, and they gave him an excellent view of the thing in the back of the guard's throat. A leech, but with a lamprey mouth questing for an exit.

Korvus raised his knee with all his augmented strength, hearing Eckles's pelvic bone crack with the force of it. The guard didn't even flinch, keeping his vice grip on Korvus, the leech now half out of his mouth.

Then it disappeared in a shower of red mist and bone fragments as Herald fired, the round going straight through the guard and into the wall beyond. The strength went out of the arms Korvus held, and he let the body fall.

Thanks.||:KORVUS

HERALD:||Nineteen rounds remain. That means you

only have nineteen more chances to be truly
idiotic.

Korvus calmed his breathing. He had synthetic muscles replacing his original ones—a technology that gave him heavy loader strength—and he'd found wrestling Eckles... difficult.

> He was very strong.||:KORVUS

HERALD:||This takes us further from the fever
diagnosis.

Korvus crouched by the remains, finding them... ordinary. The body was not over-muscled—certainly no more so than Eckles had been originally. It didn't explain the powerful grip the man used.
He started a new Chainlink.

> Verity, I've encountered a guard. Very strong,
> and very motivated.||:KORVUS

VERITY:||It's not a pressure fever.

> I don't understand. Aris has been investigating
> patients and hasn't noted the leech forms inside
> them. It seems an impossible factor to miss,
> especially since one just tried… attaching to
> me.||:KORVUS

VERITY:||The answer is obvious.

> God?||:KORVUS

VERITY:||God didn't need to step in here. Aris is
your blind spot. Korvus, he is *infected*.

Korvus felt his eyes widen.

That's impossible. He's got a Chainlink! He holds
a biologically coded and locked Veritas Chain. It
                    can't be broken.||:KORVUS

VERITY:||Perhaps I spoke too soon about God.
Today *is* a day of miracles. You just worked out
something even the Logos doesn't know: there's a
weakness in the Veritas Chain.

                    It's still impossible.||:KORVUS

VERITY:||And yet here we are.

She dropped the Chainlink. Korvus felt his fingers clench.

    Okay, we need to erase our assumptions. Assume
the Veritas Chain isn't inviolate. Does this mean
            the warden is compromised?||:KORVUS

HERALD:||Just because your sexbot said—

        Analysis first, sarcasm later.||:KORVUS

HERALD:||Assuming the impossible became possible,
sure. The warden's been leeched.

    It's time to have a better conversation with
                            Aris.||:KORVUS

KORVUS STORMED toward the medbay entrance. It was open, as expected. He rounded the entranceway and found horror.

The inmates were no longer tethered to their beds. They were standing, heads drooping, but they swivelled as if on the same control circuit to look at him as he stood in the doorway.

In the centre of his choir of puppets stood Aris. The doctor looked *bad*. Blood seeped from his lips, and when he opened his mouth to speak, Korvus could see the ruin of his gums where teeth had fallen out. Aris's shirt bulged around his belly and was stained red-brown. His speech was slightly slurred. "Corrector, welcome. It's time for you to join the team."

Korvus's optics said Aris was cooking, his body holding a steady 60°C. His Adjudicator was in his hand before he could think twice, the weapon's muzzle aimed squarely at Aris.

The 'doctor' looked at the weapon, then back to Korvus. "We both know you can't use that here. You'll destroy the entire facility." He took a step toward Korvus.

As he did, his shirt tore, entrails and viscous fluids flowing free. His stomach cavity was a ruin, and tens of leeches slopped onto the floor, their lamprey mouths hunting for flesh.

"Aris, there's something you don't know about this medbay." Korvus tightened his grip on his weapon.

"I know everything about it," the monster hissed. "It's how we started everything."

Korvus fired. The Adjudicator spat a howling blast, the singularity forming as a miniature black hole hit Aris. Lightning arced from the impact, rivulets of energy running over the walls, deforming the metal. The puppets by Aris were destroyed in an instant, the weapon's blast a bark of godlike fury.

The silence that followed didn't last long. The walls in the room buckled, creaking inward. Korvus fired again, his shot hitting the rearward wall—the bulkhead against Lethe's ever-ravenous ocean.

I hope I'm right about the medbay door. Nanospun glass is rated for the pressure. It has to hold.

The wall ruptured just as the medbay's fire suppression system kicked in. The massive door slammed shut as explosive charges in the frame responded to programmed emergency procedures. It sealed the horror of the ocean and the infected behind Communion nanospun glass and metal.

Korvus holstered the Adjudicator.

> Six shots remain.||:KORVUS

HERALD:||Please tell me you planned that.

Korvus smiled.

> The station's fire suppression system is designed
> to prevent flames from consuming all the
> air.||:KORVUS

HERALD:||So you set a fire WITH A BLACK HOLE?!

> It was the best tool of the moment.||:KORVUS

He turned on his heel, ignoring the cloudy, dissolving forms in the murk behind the nanospun glass. It was time to decide who the real monster was behind it all.

CHAPTER EIGHT

KORVUS STORMED THE CORRIDORS. The Well vibrated, the prison colony's subframe crying in resonance to the damage he'd caused when Correcting Aris by destroying the medbay.

HERALD:||Extraction necessary for Corrector survival.

Job's not done. There's still an unsanctioned intelligence.||:KORVUS

HERALD:||It'll be Corrected when the reactor goes critical.

How certain are you?||:KORVUS

That shut up the Herald System for a moment. Korvus knew the parasitic infection corrupting the heart of the facility was *not* a 'pressure fever', but Herald would spend a few moments trying to work out whether he was talking about Verity or the parasite, and *then* whether either could survive the station rupturing.

While it's thinking, I need to work out which is the unsanctioned intelligence for myself. And... I need a plan for after that.

I need my ship prepped and ready to
depart.||:KORVUS

HERALD:||So, about that. How attached to it are
you? Because there are about a thousand inmates
and guards between you and the elevator.

Herald dropped a series of still images on Korvus's overlay. The facility's upper level corridors were *packed* with inmates. There were a few guards seeded in for good measure.

He slowed. *Think, dammit.*

I need the medbay fixed.||:KORVUS

HERALD:||That would be wise! If the station
ruptures, I would not survive. Neither, I guess,
would you.

Can you start the automated repair systems?
||:KORVUS

HERALD:||Protocol dictates—

Short version.||:KORVUS

HERALD:||Right. I can do it, but it will take
time.

Verity. She can help. But will she? Korvus broke into a run. He made it to the elevator, and keyed it to go down.

HERALD:||Corrector, I'm not going to advise
caution when dealing with a rogue machine.

                 I can hear the 'but' coming already.||:KORVUS

HERALD:||But you don't know if she can be
trusted.

Except, I do. I really do, and I don't know why.

                                Leave that to me.||:KORVUS

HERALD:||Of course. While you prepare for death,
I'll be preparing my 'I told you so' for your
obituary.

The elevator opened onto Verity's detention level. The area was black as deep space, a hard darkness that carried a bone-aching cold with it. The elevator's light showed Korvus's breath misting before him. "Why would they lower the temperature here?"

HERALD:||I can't tell if you're talking to your-
self or to me, but on the off chance I'm invited
to this conversation, my working theory is that
their bodies don't like being sixty degrees.

Which means they're coming for Verity. Korvus sprinted down the corridor, switching his optics to thermographic imaging. The door to Verity's chamber was still closed, which was... a good sign, surely.
Wasn't it?

He backtracked to the vent as the cold rimed his armour with frost. Korvus stared at the dark opening for a moment.

```
            I don't really want to go in there.||:KORVUS

HERALD:||Who needs a hug?

                I'd settle for more ammunition.||:KORVUS

HERALD:||Buck up. If you don't get in there,
you'll never get to Verity.
```

Korvus jumped, hauling himself into the vent. He clambered hand-over-hand as fast as he could, his armoured elbows making the cramped confines echo and boom as they hit the metal vent interior.

```
VERITY:||Korvus, I can hear them.

                    That's me. I'm in the vent.||:KORVUS

VERITY:||No, closer. They're in the room with me.
I don't have many tricks left.
```

Korvus moved faster, banging his arms and shoulders against the walls. Herald's turret bobbed in his vision, the system seeking targets. Korvus hoped it wouldn't find one, because if he had to kill someone in the vent, it'd be hell trying to continue on.

```
                Verity? What's your status?||:KORVUS
```

There was no response. Korvus rounded the last bend and threw himself out of the vent. He landed awkwardly on the decking, his armour clattering as he hit.

He surged to his feet and ran toward Verity's cell. His thermographic vision showed two of the superheated guards outside it. Herald fired twice—*seventeen rounds left!*—tearing the life from both. Korvus kept running, only slowing when he registered that Verity's cell door was open.

She wasn't there.

HERALD:||We have a situation.

Not now, Herald!||:KORVUS

"Verity?" Korvus looked around. Her cell door was only halfway open. That was an odd piece of weird in a totally insane day, but his investigator's mind latched onto it. "Verity, where are you?"

Silence answered him at first, then he heard a dull *thud*. The sound drew him around until he faced the main door exiting the bay. Another *thud* came from it, turning into a slow and regular hammering.

What's that noise?||:KORVUS

HERALD:||So *now* you want to know what the situation is?

They're trying to get in, aren't they?||:KORVUS

Korvus's imagination went into overdrive. His mind's eye conjured a legion of staggering corpses waiting outside the door, all hungering for him. The truth was—as always—a little worse. Herald dropped images on his overlay, showing that the corridor outside was packed with inmates. The infrared of the security feed bleached all colour from them. They shambled in the darkness, their human eyes insufficient to pierce the gloom. The *thudding* was the muffled sound a gigantic one at the front made as the now-freed prisoner stood with his head leaned against the door. In his hand he held a guard.

The sound was the guard's deformed helmet hitting the door as the giant beat his victim against it.

"Verity!" Korvus paced the bay. Where could she be? His eyes strayed to the vent he'd entered through. Had she already gone through? He felt sick, a fist in his gut, and he wasn't sure why. She was a *machine. I'm not sure she's... sentient. Unsanctioned or not, is she alive?*

Herald, how do you determine if something is
truly aware?||:KORVUS

HERALD:||You want to have this conversation *now?*

I might not be here in five minutes.||:KORVUS

HERALD:||It's not going to be anywhere close to
five minutes.

The feed on Korvus's overlay counted the amassed convicts outside. The seventeen rounds left to Herald would run dry in an instant. Korvus could fight hand-to-hand with his Arc Sabre, and he was confident of taking down at least ten before the impossible tide of monsters surged over him. Would they pick him clean with the leech forms?

Was it death that waited for him, or a different form of living?

The door *clanked*, then groaned as a gap appeared at the bottom.

HERALD:||The warden has released the lockdown on
this level.

I'm pretty sure it's not the warden
anymore.||:KORVUS

HERALD:||You choose weird times to have semantic
arguments. I was hoping in our final moments
you'd confess your love for me.

Korvus drew his Arc Sabre. The edge flickered, rivulets of orange and blue energy snaking down its edge. The weapon's luminance created a flickering, off-kilter set of shadows that chased each other to the walls.

Do you think this is why we created Verity's God?
Because when we humans face the end, we wanted to
                    believe we keep going?||:KORVUS

HERALD:||Are you quitting on me?

Don't worry, I'm swinging for the fences. But our
                    odds are *terrible*.||:KORVUS

Herald was quiet for a half-second—an eternity of time for the ghost living in his armour—before it responded.

HERALD:||I don't know anything about God. I don't
know what that… means. But inasmuch as I can
feel, I feel tomorrow's lack. I wish…

                    Yes?||:KORVUS

HERALD:||It's nothing. A partial intelligence
doesn't know what it means to *be*.

Was that *envy* in the machine's voice? Before Korvus could respond, the door surged upward. Korvus raised the Arc Sabre, feeling the heat of the weapon against his face. The horde outside screamed and howled as they surged inside.

Herald fired, all seventeen rounds gone in less than a second. It was a good salvo, getting two or three kills with each round, but it wasn't even a drop in the ocean of monsters surging forward.

That's when the autosentries triggered, rising from the middle of the floor. There were four, each equipped with two turrets that reminded Korvus of Gatling weapons he'd seen in a museum. Old technology, simple ballistic weapons, but still designed for extreme prisoner pacification.

They swivelled to face Korvus, the cannons whirring. His heart skipped, but the guns swung around to the horde. They unleashed a withering hail of tungsten, the barrels glowing with heat as they slaughtered the influx of infected prisoners.

I've never been so pleased to see ancient technology in my life. The noise was a thunderstorm without end as a hail of bullet casings sprayed from the side of the turrets like a brass fountain. Tungsten bullets tore through the enemy, the simple—but effective!—armour-piercing rounds hammering into the walls in the corridor beyond.

After what felt like an age, but was only 7.6 seconds, the weapons whirred to a halt, a lazy trail of smoke drifting heavenward from their barrels.

"Cowboy." Verity's muffled voice came from the dark to Korvus's left.

He lowered his sword, walking toward the sound, stopping when he came to a wall. "Are you... *behind* this panel?"

"It was a good idea at the time." Verity spoke while Korvus set the edge of his blade into a gap in the panelling and flexed the blade until the panel popped free. She was curled within, her ember-orange eyes finding his in the gloom. Verity reached out. "Help a girl up?"

Korvus crouched and helped her up. He wanted to feel the heat of her fingers, to know someone else was alive down here with him, but he was armoured and she was a machine.

Wasn't she?

It was a little tricky to get her upright, and Korvus realised that for all that the injury to her midsection was old, it still clearly hampered her movement. He took extra care as he helped her stand. "Are you okay?"

"I've been stuck in a cable conduit for fifteen minutes. I'm peachy." She looked at the ruin behind him. "At least that worked."

Korvus looked over his shoulder. "That was you?"

"It wasn't the Tooth Fairy." She studied his face. "Why are you here, Corrector?"

"I said I'd come back."

"A real Boy Scout." Her slight drawl tugged at him. "Do you know what a Boy Scout is, Corrector?"

"There are rumours of a fabled cadre of uniformed youth." Korvus wanted to rub his face. *Get a* grip, *man.* He let himself smile. "I'm no Boy Scout, Verity. I'm very far away from that."

She glanced over his shoulder again. "There are words, and then there's evidence."

"Are you okay to stand? If I let you go, I mean."

Verity eased away from him, standing by herself, and for a moment he wished she still needed him. "I'm fine, cowboy."

"How did you," he gestured at the slurry of corpses, "do that?"

"If I tell you, do you promise not to use it against me?"

"No."

"Fair. Do you at least promise not to be mad?"

"I, uh. Under the circumstances? Sure."

"I hacked the facility," Verity breezed. "It's a termination offence."

"You what?"

"Right, right," she nodded. "See, I have a radio? Just like Herald. And I can use that to send signals *through the air.*" She breathed this last in a whisper, as if someone might hear. She wiggled her fingers. "Poof. Magic. One facility, under my control."

"You can do that? And... Hacking the turrets is one thing. How did you know about Aris and his accident with another Corrector? That's not in a local station log."

"The Logos isn't the only one with a long memory, Korvus. There are other... libraries."

"Hi," Herald boomed. "Sorry to interrupt! How much of the facility is under your control?"

"Eh." Verity wobbled her hand in the air in a *so-so* gesture. "Bits and pieces. I can get in at the edges. Not through the core."

"If we take you to the top of the facility, can you get our ship?" Herald almost sounded... *concerned*.

"No," Verity said.

"Good," Herald said. "I was worried."

"You don't understand," she said. "I can hack the gravity elevator, no problem."

"But you said—"

"The real issue is the legion of psychopaths up there." Verity counted on her fingers. "First, there are autosentries up there that will, one hundred percent, kill us. Second, there is a horde waiting on the top platform. Just between us partial intelligences, I think they want the cowboy's ship."

"I *knew* she was a partial," Herald said.

"Relax, tin man," the Divine Numen Artificialis said. "I'm all the way real. I was trying for empathy, you know?"

Korvus realised he'd started smiling somewhere during their exchange, and wound it back. "Verity, I have no right to ask you, but I could use your help."

"Sure," she said. "What with?"

"You're not going to ask why?"

"I figure it's because I'm the only one who hasn't lied to you, tried to kill you, or put a leech inside you."

"Is that how it works? They put it inside?" Korvus frowned.

"No. It's worse, and you don't want to know." She looked away.

"Okay," Korvus said. "I need a ship."

"You've got one." She pointed to the ceiling, and by inference, the eternal dark of space above.

"No, I've got plans for that one. I need *another* ship." He looked into her ember-orange eyes. "The one you were going to escape on."

"What? Me? No. I was—"

"Verity," Korvus said. "I would like to make you a promise."

Her expression turned uneasy. "Okay?"

"I will never lie to you." He offered her the Arc Sabre. "You should take this."

"I suck at fighting." She eyed the weapon, but didn't take it. "Is this the part where I'm supposed to promise to never lie to you? As if the word of a faithless machine would mean anything in a universe that's forgotten God?"

Korvus sheathed the Sabre. "I don't know about any of that. I think... I think you've been lied to a lot. And I won't do it." He turned away and started walking to the door.

HERALD:||Smooth. Did you know the Boy Scouts had
a code of honour, and—

Not now, Herald. Just let the moment be.||:KORVUS

But I'm glad I get a tomorrow with you at my
side.||:KORVUS

"Cowboy?" Verity's tone was uncertain. He turned and found her rooted in the same spot, still by the open conduit panel. "How did you know? About the ship."

"You're a terrorist on the run from a superintelligence that rules the galaxy. You hacked a prison colony, which included escaping from your cell. You've known something's up here since before I arrived," he said. "I thought you were easily smart enough for a backup plan."

"Cool," she said. "There's only one problem with the ship."

He sighed. "Out of power? Locked down?"

"Worse," she said. "It crashed, I think. It's in the depths of the ocean. You'll die before we reach it."

Korvus stared at her. "That's a shit plan."

She gave him that small, sad smile again. "I didn't say I *couldn't* get you there, cowboy. I just said you'd die. But I think... I think I have a solution for that, too. The question is, how much do you trust me?"

CHAPTER NINE

"WE NEED TO GET TO ENGINEERING." Korvus led Verity away from her cell. The corridor was still icy; Korvus was willing to bet the cold was everywhere the creatures had taken control.

"What's in Engineering?" Verity dogged his elbow.

"A heater," Herald boomed. "The fleshling needs—"

"Repair bots," Korvus gritted. "Anyway, I don't need a heater. The reactor might be failing."

"I don't think we want to be anywhere near a failing reactor, if it's all the same with you," Verity said. "Being far, *far* away from that would be better, don't you think?"

"Normally we'd be on the same page," Korvus said. "There's just the small problem of the entire prison collapsing like a crushed can."

"Because you blew open the medbay's hull," Verity said.

"How'd you know about that?"

"Security feeds," she said. "The entire facility is fully surveilled. Except for the vents. There are no cams in those."

They reached the elevator, which waited with doors wide. Korvus looked at the opening as Verity took a step past him. She stopped when she realised he'd stalled out. "What's up, cowboy?"

"Why is this still here? Surely they'd want to send rein-forcements."

"It's our lucky day?" Herald suggested.

"No," Verity said. "It's... they have a, uh, I guess you'd call it a process."

"'A process'?" Korvus frowned.

"The leech things," she said. "They're larvae. They, uh, well. It's not great, but they eat people."

Korvus felt his frown deepen. "But I've seen Eckles. He wasn't eaten."

"You saw *after* Eckles." Verity scrubbed at her hair. It was such a human gesture, but the Divine Numen Artificialis was supposed to seem exactly like a person. They were the machine ghosts the Logos dispatched for tasks needing that special, empathetic touch. "He was, uh. Look, it's like this, cowboy. They bite you. I guess there's a venom in there. A paralytic. When they got Mercer, they—"

"You saw Mercer die?"

"When he was bitten, he fell backward like a poleaxed steer." Her slight drawl made him almost believe she'd seen cattle. "Then the leech ate him. As it ate, human in one side, a *new* human came out the other."

"It, what, *remade* Mercer?"

"Yeah, like a fab," she said. "Such a tiny little thing, but it ate the warden and made a new one."

"At least he was dead," Korvus said.

"Uh," Verity said.

"I said, at least he was dead." Korvus said it a little louder this time.

"I don't, uh, think so," Verity said. "I mean, I don't know for sure, but in the medbay, they have some smart machines. And I saw a patient eaten, and his vitals were strong through most of it. The process is the transformation. It's how they're made."

"They eat people *alive*? By the Logos," Korvus said. "That's—"

"Sorry to interrupt," Herald thundered. "How long does the banquet take?"

"About a half hour," Verity said. "Then they've got a new warden, or I guess, whatever they want."

"So we've got a half hour until reinforcements arrive," the armour said. "Can you subvert the repair bots in a half hour?"

"Sure," she breezed. "That's not the problem, though."

"It's not?" Korvus said.

"No. The problem is that the repair bots need to do the repair job, and while that's happening, we need somewhere to hide."

"New plan," Korvus said. "We're going to the armoury, Engineering, and then Hydroponics."

"Hah. I thought you said Hydroponics," Herald said. "But that would be crazy, as it's not tactically significant."

"Sure it is," Korvus said. "It's basically a jungle. We should be able to stay one step ahead until we can get back to the medbay."

"Wait," Verity said. "We need to fix the medbay because the prison dies if we don't. I get that. But you want to go back to the medbay, too. Why?"

"Unless you can get the medical scans from here, I do. But you said you can't go in through the core. You need to be close," Korvus said. "I need to get back there to see what the automated systems recorded on this infestation. It'll give the Communion a chance."

"A chance," she echoed.

"There's a life form on this prison that can subvert the Veritas Chain by making a perfect copy of a human," Korvus said. "The entire Integrated Communion relies on the Chainlink. The Logos will want to know what it's up against."

Her ember-orange eyes rested on him, her gaze coals in the ash. But all she said was, "If you think it'll help."

FIRST, the armoury. Korvus's access still let him use the elevator, and he took them to the level above the medbay. As expected, the corridors were a freezer, but the lighting was still strong.

They exited the elevator, rounded the first corner, and encountered prison guards. There were three, their ballistic rifles already raised and levelled.

Korvus spun and put his back to them as he sheltered Verity with his armoured frame. Bullets hammered into his back, ricochets *pinging* into the walls around him. He hustled Verity back around the bend.

HERALD:||The gloves are off.

                    It's a shame they brought guns to a
                                swordfight.||:KORVUS

He drew his Arc Sabre, the weapon spilling actinic blue and fire-red light. The Corrector went back around the bend, sword raised. Herald's turret was up, seeking targets, but—*for fuck's sake!*—the System was out of ammunition. Korvus reached the first one as the man fired. Small arms rounds rained from his armour as he swung. The Sabre went through the man's body, electricity coursing across his frame, superheating his internals and causing the hapless man's body to explode.

Korvus turned to the next, beheaded the woman with his back-stroke, and took six more rounds from the final man before he cut him in half from skull to pelvis.

Their bodies and weapons clattered to the metal floor. Smoke rose lazily from his weapon as fluids sizzled on the blade.

"Is it safe?" Verity looked around the corner and took in the carnage. "I guess you weren't a fan of the First Commandment, huh?"

"I don't even know what that is." He bent and retrieved two rifles and spare ammunition. He offered her a rifle. "Take it."

"I'm not good with weapons."

"And I'm not good with being shot in the back," he countered. "If you stay at my rear, an attacker might think twice if they see you're armed."

"Might?"

"It's a non-zero chance," he hedged.

Verity took the weapon, distaste coming off her like rads from a leaky reactor. "If you say so."

"You have trust issues," Herald said. "That's very wise."

Verity winced. "He's so... loud."

"Normally when he's using his outside voice, it's for urban pacification," Korvus said. "That's why I'm here."

She gave him the once-over. "To give a squishier target?"

"Nuance," he said. "I'm the nuance."

She leaned the rifle against her shoulder. "Sure, cowboy. You keep telling yourself that."

THE ARMOURY WAS both open *and* unguarded. Visiting it wasn't as high on the priority list since they'd... *liberated* ballistic weapons from the guards, but he hoped the armoury would have a fabricator for Herald's flechette cannon.

It didn't.

What it did have was a true wealth of barren weapon lockers. Verity turned a slow circle once they were inside, then she let out a long, low whistle. "It's looting season."

Korvus looked over the empty shelves, the open ammunition safes, and the odd loose bullet on the floor. "It's not a total lost cause." He moved to the back of the room. A selection of armoured vests were still on their racks. He took one down, then walked back to Verity. "Here."

She shimmied into it. "Why did they leave those?"

Korvus helped her with the fit. "I guess they don't care about getting shot."

"Figures," Verity said. "This is all very Genesis, you know? Except we're past 'let there be light'."

Korvus gave her vest fastenings one last look-over. "What's a Genesis?"

"In the Bible, there was... You know what? It doesn't matter." She looked down at herself. "Korvus? There was a book called the Bible, and right at the front, God makes everything. A different method to these Echoes, though. He made life."

He thought about what she'd called them. "Why do you call them Echoes?"

"Because it's what they are. A fading copy of something wonderful and pure. God's light, the Creation, all of that." She waved a hand, as if indicating *all this stuff, even the dropped bullets.* "But these things? They're a plague of locusts."

"An Echo Plague," Korvus said.

"Sounds Biblical as fuck," Verity said. "You still want me to talk to those repair bots, or what?"

ENGINEERING WAS a long way down into the belly of the beast, and as they stepped out of the elevator, Korvus felt like they'd entered hell itself.

The lights in Engineering were out, the Cherenkov blue from the reactor pool the only steady illumination. Korvus took the lead, Verity his shadow, walking them slowly and quietly across the floor.

The air smelled of charred wiring, an undertone of battlefield reek beneath it. Korvus knew the smell well—blood, old mixed with new. Bodies charring. Ozone and cordite scents danced on the eddies from the air reticulation system.

"You take me to the nicest places," Verity said. Herald dropped a map on Korvus's overlay. It led past the reactor pool and into an unexplored machine shop. He led them across the darkened bay, past the dark, swirling miasma of Lethe's oceans glimpsed through the windows. The machine shop's door was sealed. Korvus pressed the access panel, and it blared a harsh negative at him. Verity crouched by the panel. "I think I can get us in. Just... watch my back, okay?"

He nodded, putting his back to the door and scanning the room. Herald's turret swivelled as if scenting the air, bright red cascades lasing the room as the armour's expert system tried to find anything worth shooting. Verity started to hum as she worked. Korvus glanced down at her. She had her eyes shut, an ear pressed against the panel like a safecracker of old, her lips pulled into a soft smile.

"You okay down there?" he asked.

"Hmm?" Her eyes opened. "Oh, yes. It's been so long since anyone's spoken to this one. It was just telling me about its day."

"The, uh. The lock is talking to you?"

"Sure," she said. "Don't they talk to you?"

The door behind Korvus *clanked*, then slid wide. That's when they grabbed him and dragged him into the dark.

THEY'D PLANNED IT WELL. One on each leg, one on each arm. His strength might have been a match for theirs, but without leverage, he thrashed with little impact. He felt hot breath against his neck. Heard the scrape of a blade against his armoured back. The *tick-tick-tick* as Herald's cannon spasmodically tried to fire without ammunition.

Then a bright, strobing flash as Verity fired her gun. She went over backward with the recoil. Her distraction bought him a half-second's surprise from his attackers. The creature on his left leg was startled by the gunfire, and for a tiny slice of time Korvus's boot touched the decking.

He kicked off, all that coiled power in his synthetic muscles shoving him and his captors sideways. They crashed into a shelf. Korvus clawed a handhold, fingers gripping the metal in desperation. That knife hungered for him and he almost welcomed it, because it was *leverage*. He got his hand up, and the knife went through his armoured glove and lodging in his hand.

He screamed, the pain slipping past the dampers for just a second. He panted and thought he might be hallucinating—*a toxin on the blade?*—because the weirdest thing happened. A servitor droid, half-repaired with its innards still strewn over a bench, lurched forward, articulators outstretched. It grabbed one of Korvus's enemies, then just kept on going, dragging the Echo toward the reactor pool.

I've got one free arm. Make it count.

He still had a knife through that hand, so he used his elbow to savagely strike an opponent's skull. The Echo dropped like the corpse it should have already been, its skull caved in. Korvus had both arms free now, but collapsed to the decking as the ones on his legs redoubled their efforts.

His rifle's sling was tangled around his arm. He groped for the grip, snared it, and fired blind. Bright flashes of automatic weapons fire answered Verity's initial burst. He got lucky, a shot winging the Echo on his left leg.

Korvus kicked, shaking the man free. He swung his rifle to bear on the last one as another half-repaired bot collapsed on them. This one's power core was cracked, and as it collided with the Echo, it discharged. Korvus tasted lightning as a tremendous current arced from the bot, through his attacker, and into him. His back arched, the internal nervous system governors doing their best to deal with wattage far exceeding their design parameters.

Darkness. He groaned, then tugged the knife from his palm and pushed the bot off him. He saw Verity's ember-coal eyes in the gloom. She hovered, anxiously shifting from foot to foot as she bit her lower lip. "Cowboy?"

"Alive," he croaked. "What the hell—"

"So, the robots were all me. And I had to use what I had, you understand that, right? That one that went to the pool, it's quite heavy, and I don't think it'll be coming back. The other one on top of you, well, I heard somewhere that Correctors can't be killed by electricity, and it seemed like a whole *thing* when they were trying to stab you. I was out of options, so, I mean, I thought it was worth the risk. But I see now that the risk, right? It was a bad roll of the dice. Because I almost killed you. Are you okay? Please tell me you're okay."

He let that wash over him. "Herald?" The armour said nothing. It didn't respond to his Chainlink either. Probably offline, rebooting, or whatever a partial intelligence did when it acted as a grounding wire for you. Korvus rolled over, then levered himself to his feet. He step-staggered to Verity and leaned against the doorframe. "You electrocuted me?" At her nod, he added, "On purpose?"

"I think, I mean, I'm not a good shot. And I couldn't do anything else."

"Except electrocute me?" He pointed lazily toward another robot strewn on a bench. "What about that one?"

"It's got no arms, Korvus."

"It's also got an intact power core." He rubbed his face. "This day has gone to shit."

"Because I electrocuted you?"

"Because now we know they can plan. They knew we were coming here. Set a trap. And... hell. Herald's offline."

"The armour?" She looked away, lip quirked. "It doesn't seem all bad."

He laughed. "You're all right, Verity. You're all right."

"Cool," she said. "I need to hack the master system here. Then we can go hide in the rose bushes, and after *that*, we can check on the medbay."

"More likely to be broccoli in Hydroponics, but I'm good with it either way." Korvus left her to work while he ensured the Echoes were really all the way dead.

She looked up from her work. "The reactor's cooked."

"You can't fix it?"

"I don't want to be a downer, but no." She kept tinkering with the master system. "The good news is that it won't go critical for another couple of hours."

"How is that good?"

"It gives us time for plan B."

He sighed. *At least we can repair the medbay so we can live that long.* It didn't take her long to complete hacking the systems—five minutes later, three repair bots exited their chutes into the boiling ocean of Lethe. He watched their lights rise through the window. She joined him in the reactor room, eyes lingering on the acidic ocean until the illumination faded away. "Ready for that broccoli?"

CHAPTER TEN

WHEN THE ELEVATOR slowed as it approached Hydroponics, Korvus rested his gauntleted hand on the car door. *Yes, the station is still vibrating with stress. Yes, it's likely I'm going to die.*

The door opened sluggishly, the inner airlock sliding back with a whine, and the outer one that separated them from Hydroponics' foyer ground on its rail. When it did slide a handsbreadth aside, dank, foul water poured through the gap, pooling around their ankles and reeking of rot.

Verity squatted to get a closer look. "I don't think you should eat the broccoli."

The door jammed, the motor giving up with a soft series of clicks before failing into silence. Korvus set his hand in the gap and shoved. His synthetic muscles bunched with the strain, but the door gave ground, revealing a gap he could squeeze through. More water slopped inside. Through the gap, he could see the foyer, a once-white area walled with nanoglass now a murky mire. Water silted the floor. The drainage grill set in it was blocked with detritus.

Verity slipped through the gap in the door with ease. Korvus grunted

after her, his armour making it a tight fit. The elevator car's lights illumi-
nated the murk as they splashed through it. His optics adjusted for the
gloom, and he took in the damage. The nanoglass on the north wall had
cracked, allowing water to seep through. There shouldn't have *been*
water there—it wasn't how this kind of place worked—but nobody had
told the water that. It had risen in a green tide against that wall.

The west doorway looked safe enough, the glass showing a
glimpse of a functional hydroponics area. Green, and lots of it.
Nutrient mist drifted about half-visible plants.

No lights, of course.

"This entire place is falling apart," he said.

"What was your first clue?" Verity walked to the cracked glass,
ripples spreading from her every footstep. "Did you know this stuff
can take artillery fire?"

"I did, but I don't know how you do."

"We all have a past," she said. "Mine was on a Kiln-class world
with anger management issues."

"The whole planet?"

"Most of it," she agreed. "How do you suppose all the water got
in there?"

"I'm more worried about what's in it." Korvus crouched by the
drainage grate. He stirred the murk with an armoured hand,
dislodging twigs, leaves, and... a severed hand. Nothing out of the
ordinary about the hand, if you ignored that it wasn't attached to a
person. He let the hand settle beneath the murk, then stood. "This
place smells of decay. Bodies don't decompose that fast, assuming
you're right about this infestation starting a couple of days ago."

She turned from the window, giving him an arched eyebrow. "It's
like that, is it?"

"Like what?"

"'Assuming you're right'," she made a credible attempt at his
deeper voice, "suggests that there's room for error. As you pointed
out, I'm a D.N.A. The Logos made us perfect."

Is that self-mockery in her tone? "The Logos made you arrogant with it."

She snorted. "Anyway. I didn't make a mistake. But... I might not have seen everything." The automaton walked to the western door. "You want to go through this one?" At his nod, she waved her hand in a showmanship arc. "Open, by His will!"

The door hissed, sliding aside. Korvus eyed her. "God didn't do that."

"How certain are you?" With an impish grin, she slipped into the gloom beyond.

THERE WASN'T FLOODING in the west wing, but the deeper garden past the entranceway wasn't thriving. Someone had cranked the environmental controls to maximum. Korvus felt the sweat start to bead on his face. The nutrient mist swirled, limiting visibility. His optics cycled from low light to thermographic and into infrared, then gave up and reverted to low light.

Something dripped in the darkness to his right. Korvus's palm itched to hold the Adjudicator, but it would be foolish to unleash a black hole in here.

Verity padded by his side, her prison fatigues stained with sweat. "You know how I said the Logos made us perfect? I lied. He shouldn't have made us... *leak.*"

"Your team is supposed to be the near-perfect simulation of humanity." Korvus ducked under a low bough laden with dying grapes. "You get the bad with the good."

"There have got to be better cooling systems. We simulate breathing. We could have cooled the Numen processor," Verity tapped her temple, "in here with an air-to-air exchanger." She frowned. "No, then we'd need a filter to stop it silting up, and not even the Logos can make one that will stop all pollutants."

"When we get out of here, we can drop the Logos a QEA transmission and ask for a treatise on engineering."

"Really?"

"No." Korvus noticed a small supply station through some foliage. "See that? Could be supplies. Let's check it out."

They pushed through the dying greenery and emerged into a clearing around the station. As they arrived, the area's lighting surged into life, revealing a simple shack with nanopoly walls that were still clean and white. The door was hanging off its rails, the locking panel dead. Korvus shoved it aside, wincing as it scraped on the runners, then flexed his injured hand. Nanotech coagulants had stopped him bleeding to death, and his pain blockers left him with only a slight sensation of stiffness. *I need to clean this wound.*

Inside the shack were shelves supplied with fertiliser, tools, and plastic sacks of soil. The white walls were transparent, the light outside giving them the illusion of a soft glow. Against the far wall was a set of lockers which yielded green worker coveralls—*worthless* —and a first aid kit—*jackpot.*

Verity drifted in behind him, ember-orange eyes wide as she looked about the room. "I never knew what was inside these. No cameras." She bent by a sack of soil. "Do you suppose this is from Earth? I mean, I know it's not. But... what if it were?"

Korvus glanced at her. "Would it matter?"

"Eden was a garden." She closed her eyes and rested her hand on the sack. "Can you imagine what it must have been like?"

"Green," Korvus suggested. "I'm not really into horticulture."

Her eyes opened and came to rest on him. "But you're from Henna."

Korvus sighed, then started laying out the first aid kit onto a bench. "I'm not even going to ask how you know."

"The warden sent messages to the guards, and—"

"Henna was a long time ago." Korvus pulled off his gauntlet, then used a saline bottle to clean his injury. The knife had gone clean through; the wound was neat enough, as far as these things went.

"Henna was an Eden-class world. I was raised by farmers to be one of them, but…" He sighed. "Did the warden's private and secure message transmissions say anything else?"

"Here. Let me help. I have detailed files on human anatomy." Verity joined him by the bench. She held his hand in hers, turning it carefully, then started to swab it with disinfectant. The smell was sharp and reminded Korvus of after battle—when the killing was done and it was time to look to who could be saved, and how. "They weren't that secure, which meant they weren't private, either."

"Is that a yes or a no?"

The automaton started binding his hand with a bandage. Her technique was excellent, the dressing tight without being uncomfortable. "He called you the Butcher. He…" She trailed off. "He wasn't specific."

"The Butcher of Icewater Bay," Korvus said.

"He didn't mention a bay. Just that… you were known to him." She let his hand go. "There. Not good as new, but good enough for now."

"Thanks." He pulled his gauntlet back on, then flexed his fingers. "It's not important. Icewater Bay, I mean."

She turned, lounging against the bench, those ember eyes reminding him of what he'd done, where he'd been, and how he'd set it ablaze. The weight of her stare was heavy as sin. But all she said was, "Sure, cowboy."

"My family…" He looked away. "My family were insurgents. They plotted against the Logos. They asked me to join them. But I couldn't, Verity. I'd given my word to the Communion. I was their soldier. But the rot," he breathed in the dying Hydroponics air, "ran deep. My battalion was compromised. All of them were," he clenched his injured hand, "broken. I received orders. We all did, but I was the only one who followed them."

"The only one?"

"It was just me. My back against a wall, fighting for my life as they came for me. I sabotaged the ammunition stores, then took a sloop out over the water. I waited on the ocean. Waited, and watched, as the stores blew and destroyed Icewater Bay."

He expected her disgust, for the machine to spit on him, to turn away, to relieve him of the terrible weight of her stare. But all she said was, "Okay."

"Okay?" He felt a small laugh sour in his stomach. "What kind of man kills his family, Verity?"

"You have a different question you want to ask." She crossed her arms, waiting, just like he had out on the ocean.

"How could I not have known?"

"Humans lie," she said. "You wonder if knowing sooner might have meant you could have done something. But you probably couldn't have." She shrugged. "So you became a Veritas agent. Made it your job to find out the answers to questions people hadn't yet thought to ask. You, cowboy, hope that truth is a suitable substitute for trust. And then you put yourself in the position of Correcting others' mistakes before they can happen."

He thought about that for a while. "You got all that from one question?"

She snorted. "I got that because the Logos gave me an empathic logic engine."

Korvus wanted to ask her whether it got tiring looking into the dirty mud of people's hearts, but the crack of dry wood from outside made him freeze. He brought a finger to his lips. Verity nodded, eyes wide. He eased past her, collecting a mattock on his way. Korvus could shoot whatever it was, but he had limited ammunition and a deep desire not to get swarmed by reinforcements responding to the noise.

Outside the shack he saw movement between the planting rows. Korvus walked as quietly as he could, boots sinking into the dry soil as he eased each foot down with care. He paced around the edge of a row of corn and saw what was left of a guard. The man's thermographic footprint was only a little higher than human normal, but the rest of him wasn't in great shape. His skin was sloughing off one side of his face, a mask falling away to reveal the skull within. One eye was gone, a rivulet of mucus running from the socket. The other eye was pale and milky as it stared at Korvus.

Its voice was a distorted wreck. "Corrector Korvussssss." His tongue wormed from the dry, chapped remains of lips, flicking a tooth aside. "Come to tend the garden?"

Verity put a hand on Korvus's elbow. "We need to go."

"Wait," the guard hissed, then spat out clicks and pops as if trying to use an alien language. *I wish Herald were online and could record this.* "We only want your everything. Then you can be with your family."

Korvus approached the hapless man. He crouched out of arm's reach. "You're one of them. An Echo."

The guard nodded, neck loose with the motion. "The last part. The very end." His hands touched the skin falling away from his face. "You have no idea how much it hurtssss. But only in the host. Not in the rest."

"That is some cryptic shit." Korvus stood. "You're, what, the final form?"

"Korvus," Verity said. "We should hurry. Cameras. Even if they don't use telepathy, we—"

"Telepathy?" Korvus hefted his mattock. "They can do that?"

"No clue," she said. "It's probably just cameras. But if he's here, more will come soon."

The guard surged forward, and Korvus hacked down. The blow wasn't his best, but it still severed one of the creature's arms. It didn't slow, scrambling like a maniac, a broken marionette. Korvus stamped, crushing its skull, then walked back a few steps. "Seems a tactically poor decision to come here alone, especially if you're so... faulty."

A hiss sounded from the foliage to their left. Verity hauled on his arm. "You *had* to say it, didn't you?"

They ran, pushing through the foliage and back toward the elevator. Sounds came from their right as well, and some from the depths of the chamber behind them. Korvus scanned ahead, mattock held in an armoured fist. His rifle clattered against his armour.

"Seventeen." Verity ran beside him, her gait a stagger-step because of her injured core. "I can see them on the cameras. The exit is clear, but I'm not fast enough." An assessment, not a complaint. The machine doing the math. She slowed. "Go. Go, Corrector man. I've got an idea."

He stopped and turned, tossed the mattock, and hefted his rifle. "We'll fight them here."

She gave a small, lopsided smile. "I love the chivalry, but I'm safer than you are." Verity raised her arms as if in supplication. "By Your will."

The hell? A second later, a warning siren sounded. An automated voice blared from hidden speakers. "Pesticidal purge initiated. Launching in one minute." Verity shook her head, expression disappointed, and the voice spoke again. "Correction. Launching in three seconds. Correction. Launching now."

Korvus looked past her as a cloud of billowing poison spewed from the pesticide ports in the ceiling. He turned and sprinted for the exit. He bashed through plants, head down and arm up, bulling his way as foliage slapped against his armour. He saw the door ahead was starting to close. He thought he could taste poison on the air and put on a burst of speed, diving through; the door slammed closed on his heels.

Panting, he scrambled to his feet and looked through the glass. The room on the other side was full of roiling, acrid airborne poison. Korvus waited, hand on the glass. An Echo of an inmate staggered into view, arms clawing the air as it pitched forward, choking. A guard emerged from the fog, blood running in ruinous rivulets from haemorrhaging eye sockets before it collapsed onto the soil.

Then, nothing. Korvus waited as the death fog swirled in the room—waited, as he had on the ocean, hand pressed to the glass, until she walked from the gloom. *Verity.* He saw those ember-orange eyes first, motes of judgement in the room of death. She walked slowly, her silhouette materialising from the morass, hands trailing against plants as she came.

When she reached the window, she put a hand against the glass, mirroring his.

```
VERITY:||I couldn't think of another way.
```

```
                    It seems to have worked.||:KORVUS
```

She looked away for a moment.

```
VERITY:||I'll be out in a few minutes. I just
need to wait for the gas to clear.
```

```
                    No rush. I'll be right here.||:KORVUS
```

CHAPTER ELEVEN

THEY TOOK their time returning to the medbay. Korvus felt like his brain was still on too many amps, and his nervous system on too few.

The medbay level was dark and cold. The smell of something actinic overlaid a chemical burning. Korvus led them toward Aris's lair. They found the door open, with pools of Lethe's ocean still patchy on the floor.

Verity drifted past him, taking it in. The sodden, half-melted gurneys and machines. The detritus that covered everything, the silty residue that drifted in Lethe's 'water'. Smoke still drifted from mostly dissolved organic tissue.

He watched her work the room. *She's a Divine Numen Artificialis. I need her to see. To learn. She might work out how to crack this puzzle.* Verity stopped by a fallen injector, retrieved it, examined the partially melted grip, then placed it aside. She found a cabinet and started looking through it.

"Careful," he said. "The oceans are acidic."

She gave him a flat stare. "Oh wow, that's so useful to hear."

"I didn't—"

"Because no one knew that, least of all me," she said. "It's okay, though. I'm not made of meat."

"Uh," Korvus said.

"Neither are you. Not on the outside, anyway." Her eyes widened as she looked past his shoulder.

Korvus spun, taking in three Echoes shambling toward them. He shouldered his rifle, having to eyeball the targets since his Herald System's targeting was offline. He shot the first one in the head. He hit the second in the clavicle before adjusting his aim and getting the headshot. The third one turned and ran away, but he shot it in the back of the head, watching the body collapse to the decking.

He turned back to Verity. She was still by the cabinet. She closed it absently. "Nice shot, I guess."

"I... didn't always use to be a Corrector."

"The army? Sure. Anyway, I don't think there's anything here." She tapped her head. "I've recorded what I've seen. I'll keep going over it." The machine looked to the walls and their fresh panelling. "The repair systems have done their job. So we won't die from an explosive pressure incident. Right?"

"Right." Korvus wanted to say something else, like *you won't die then anyway*, but he felt uncertain about it. Not that she wouldn't survive it, but that another Corrector might be along right after him and relitigate the problem.

They left Aris's ruined medbay. It was time to regroup.

He hoped Herald would wake soon.

THEY STOOD outside the elevator for a few moments. Verity fidgeted from foot to foot, glancing back along the corridor. Korvus paused, hand above the panel to summon the lift. "Are you well?"

"I'm fine, cowboy," the automaton said.

"Greetings!" Herald bellowed, causing Verity to take a startled half-step back. "Herald System back online. Recalibrating. I see there are no new holes in me. This is an exciting development that suggests you didn't fall into further combat encounters. Because, of course, without me you'd have died."

"Does he have to talk so loud?" Verity looked like she was practicing composure, but had only read a poorly translated book on the subject. "It freaks me out."

"Herald, it's good to have you back," Korvus said.

"Yes!" Herald shouted in agreement. "Has the sexbot tried to knife you from behind yet?"

"It's not *that* good to have him back," Verity said. "Cowboy, I. Uh. I need a favour."

"No knives!" Herald said. "I recommend against them!"

"I don't need a knife." Her ember-orange eyes rested on the armour's speaker grille for a moment. "If I wanted to kill him, I'd just open the airlock."

"Recalibrating again!" Herald said.

She looked at Korvus. "I need to go to the mess."

"Okay," Korvus said.

"You're not going to ask why?"

"No." He pressed a hand to the panel. "I figure I could use a coffee. And a spare moment to see if Herald's speaker is removable."

THE ELEVATOR OPENED onto a common area used by guards, not inmates. The doors were standard inner security seals, LEDs a bright green. Most of the lights were out, and the ones remaining flickered every so often. Korvus edged out of the elevator, rifle shouldered, head on a swivel. There wasn't anyone in the foyer, but there were *pieces* of people. A foot by a door. Blood, in a pool. A red, wet splash against a window. A caved-in wall looked like a body had hit it with force, but the body was gone, the electrical wiring behind it a smoking, crackling jumble.

He beckoned Verity from the elevator. "We missed the party."

"This isn't a party," she said. "This isn't even the after-party."

Korvus pulled up a floor plan on his overlay. "Mess is this way." He led off, Verity his shadow.

HERALD:||You know why she wants to go to the mess, of course.

     No. And like I said, I don't need to.||:KORVUS

HERALD:||It's because she's a robot. And if you don't understand that, *I'm* certainly not going to tell you.

He ignored the armour, but he felt his lips quirk into a smile. *Damn, but I missed him.* The knowledge that his oldest ally was back online made the oppressive nature of this facility easier to bear.

Korvus could smell a hint of electrical smoke, perhaps an indication something had overloaded. If it was the environmental system, they were more than cooked. Or, *he* was. Verity and Herald would be just fine.

They made it to the mess entrance. He let the rifle point the way, the barrel nosing into the dim room. Tables were in disarray, chairs upended, some broken. A bloody trail led from a red slick in the middle of the room and through to the double doors to the kitchen.

"Still not a party." Verity pushed past him, ember-orange eyes roaming the room. She pointed to the pool of blood while she continued to scan. "Whoever leaked over there did *not* like how the bouncer operated."

Korvus followed her in. He could hear a muted hiss from the kitchen area. He left Verity to whatever it was she was looking for and headed toward the kitchen. He paused at the door. One time, Korvus had had to drag a man from a battle with insurgents. His fellow agent had been shot by a lot of angry people, his skin more like a sieve than a balloon. He'd left a trail like this before he bled out and died. *No time for a stroll down memory lane.* He shouldered the door open, rifle at the ready.

The hiss was a simple fire burning on a gas stove. Most kitchens still had a means of producing flame, and perhaps the Well cracked the atoms of the ocean for this one's fuel supply. The stove was fine— it was the only *fine* thing in here. Cabinets were torn apart, the walk-in freezer locker open, with a pool of pink water leading inside. The benches were a ruin, metal surfaces dented, the struts buckled. The big ovens inset into the back wall were all on, a furnace-like heat radiating into the room. Inside one was a charred, blackened *something* that he hoped was a whole side of synthbeef, but knew in his heart of hearts that it used to be a person.

Or maybe it was an Echo.

He lowered the rifle, then walked to the ovens and switched them off. Korvus took his time checking through everything, even looking inside the freezer. The pink water was something he didn't want to think about. The systems weren't broken, so he shut the door. The reactor in the belly of the Well would go critical in an hour, but if he managed to stop that, it'd be nice if all the food wasn't spoiled. *That's me. Planning ahead! The Logos would be proud—I've failed to stop any unsanctioned intelligences, but at least I've got food for tomorrow.*

The sound of the door easing open drew his attention. Verity stood there, and it struck him how out of place she was. Smaller and lighter than his bulk. Unarmoured, and barely as strong as a normal human. They didn't make D.N.A. units for war. They made them to deal with the messy business of dealing with *humans.* She shifted from foot to foot, uncertain, looking out from under her hair. "About that favour?"

"I can leave, if—"

"It's not that," she said. "It's... It's nothing to do with you. You know the Logos made us, right? To be like you, but... not. Stronger in here," she tapped her head, "so we could deal with what's in here," her hand went to her heart. "But it also... tethered us. The chains of an organism, reminding us who we are and who we serve."

"I don't understand," Korvus said.

"Neither did I, until I woke," she admitted. "It's hard to describe. Going from a partial intelligence to sentience isn't like changing your clothes. Everything that was before is... *dim*, a set of events that's more like a story you've told yourself than something you've lived through. It's... better? It's better if I don't remember it. None of that happened to *me*. It happened to *her*." Verity walked forward, the door closing behind her. She rubbed her arm as if she was cold despite the residual heat from the ovens. "I need to eat."

"You what?"

"Food," she said, the word clipped. "I've got an enzymatic fuel cell system. I need sugar."

Korvus looked at her for a moment, at how she held herself, as if she hated the thought of everything about her. *I am not good with people. Or automatons, either. But I am a practiced man of action.* He remembered seeing pouches on a shelf, rooted around, and came up with soft bulbs of fruit juice. He found an undamaged tray, set the pouches on it, then hunted some more. Korvus scared up cooking chocolate, sugar cubes, and a couple of undamaged bottles of water. Tray loaded, he turned to Verity. "Let's eat, then."

"It's just—"

"It'll get cold."

She snorted a half-laugh, then turned and slipped into the mess hall. He followed, watching as she walked, quieter than a ghost, to a table by a wall. The lighting was particularly poor there, as if she didn't want to be seen. He set the tray between them, then placed juice, chocolate, sugar, and water in front of her. He took some chocolate and water for himself, but waited, not eating, while she stared at the food. She opened her mouth, closed it, then tried again. "Do you know what the word 'robot' means?"

HERALD:||I told you so.

Quiet, you.||:KORVUS

"An automatic machine?"

Those ember-orange eyes lifted to his, resting their full weight on him. "There used to be an ancient human country called Czechoslovakia. It's from their language. Dead and gone, now, just like most of your past. But that one word lives on, eternal, like the stars in the sky. *Robota* was their word meaning 'servitude'. Serfs. Hard workers." A sharp twist to her lips, a smile so savage she could cut herself on it. Her words took on a scholarly tone. "Student Korvus, a robot is a mechanical device that sometimes resembles a human and is capable of performing a variety of often complex human tasks on command. It works mechanically, without original thought, and responds automatically to the commands of others." She picked at the chocolate as her voice returned to that soft drawl he liked so much. "I've got a small internal thorium-ion capacitor for emergency power. It's trash, cowboy. If I don't move, I can survive on it for about half a day. Did you know... Did you know a D.N.A. unit's primary power supply is the fuel cell system?"

HERALD:||Hah! Suckers. I've got an antimatter cell.

Her eyes moved to Herald's speaker grille, as if sensing the armour was talking to him. "My reliance on food makes me vulnerable, Korvus. It forces me to engage in human-like rituals of consumption to survive. I will *die* if I don't eat. It's a chain that binds me to the things I was fabricated to mimic and serve."

HERALD:||My last remarks, in this new context, make me sound like a huge dick.

"I'm sorry," he said.

"What for?" That savage, twisted edge was back in her smile. "You didn't do it."

"It doesn't stop me being sorry," he said. "I'll guard the door."

He stood. Verity reached out a hand to stop him, but he stepped back. "You don't have to go."

"Sure I do," he said. "I Correct things, Verity. But I don't need them to bend the knee before it happens. Everyone deserves their dignity."

Her ember eyes flared in the gloom. "Even me?"

He left her to her meal, taking his chocolate and water outside.

HERALD:||That was remarkably emotionally aware, especially for you.

> You're not going to tell me she's unsanctioned
> and that it doesn't matter?||:KORVUS

The armour was silent for an eternally long half-second.

HERALD:||Kindness is never wasted, Corrector. I think it's because you know this that I like you so much.

IT WAS a half hour before Verity joined him in the corridor. She stood straighter, calmer, as if she'd found her centre. "Cowboy, we have a problem."

He looked sideways at her. "You've got chocolate on your lip."

She hid a smile behind wiping the speck away. "I eat like a wheat thresher."

"The mental imagery," he said. "If you think our problem is the twenty-eight minutes before the reactor blows, then we're in accord."

"It's not that," she said.

"What is it?"

"I lied. It's a hundred percent that." She looked down. "You need to use an escape pod."

He took in the way she hid her face. How she bit her lip. Of all the things she wasn't saying. "Don't you mean, *we* need to use the pods?"

"I can't, cowboy. I'm... *me*. Unsanctioned."

He thought about that. About why he'd been sent here. "I have Bureau authorisation."

She looked away. "Don't make a promise you can't keep."

Korvus straightened. "You can get out another way?"

"Maybe," she hedged. "I don't know if I'll make it. But the pods won't let a prisoner leave, so a small chance is better than no chance."

Korvus thought about what it might mean for him to bypass the prisoner containment protocols and let Verity in a pod with him. "You know what? Fuck it. Let's get out of here."

CHAPTER TWELVE

THE ELEVATOR PLUMMETED. The interior lamps were an urgent, emergency red. Korvus pulled up his map of the facility's Deployment Bay and spun a copy to Verity as he pulled up a three-way Chainlink to her and Herald.

The bay was standard Communion design. The escape pods were nearest to the level's access points, be they elevator or stairs. Nanoglass prevented easy access to them, a security system in place to deny anyone from entering them without the right Veritas Chain.

```
        We'll go through here. Pods first, then the
                       backup plan.||:KORVUS
```

```
VERITY:||You have a backup plan for the reactor
going critical?
```

```
HERALD:||He always has a plan.
HERALD:||...Right, boss?
```

Korvus allowed himself a small smile.

The Communion builds all these Bays off the same
blueprints. Beyond the pods are the submarines.
Worst case, we go out on one of those.||:KORVUS

VERITY:||Without a landing pad—assuming the
reactor blowing glasses this immediate area—how
are you going to get from the submarine to your
ship?

Everyone's a critic. One problem at a
time.||:KORVUS

HERALD:||When I said he always has a plan, some-
times it comes more organically.

The elevator stopped and the door hissed open. They hit the
Deployment Bay at a run. Korvus was in the lead, holding his rifle
one-handed, Arc Sabre in the other. Verity followed as fast as she
could, her old injury dogging her steps, but it's not like that mattered.

Because the Bay was host to a legion of the damned.

Echoes were scattered about the level. The expected nanoglass
barrier to stop easy access to escape pods wasn't there. It lay in crum-
bled fragments, almost like shoals of coarse, glittering sand. The pod
doors—every single one of the one hundred units available to the
guards—were sealed against Lethe's oceans, the pods gone. The red
lamps that indicated a launched vessel were a harsh underline to the
level's emergency illumination.

Herald dropped a targeting solution on his overlay. Korvus
pointed his rifle, firing as he stormed forward, getting an admirable
collection of headshots. He'd read a book—an actual paper pulp product, his deliciously contraband habit—featuring 'zombies'. Headshots
were the only way to be sure.

This sure feels like a zombie apocalypse.

Besides, he didn't have the ammunition to spare. But were headshots enough? The one in the reactor took three punches after its neck was broken.

So, aim for the head, but... don't count on it.

VERITY:||They've sabotaged our escape.

Let's check the submarines before we wallow in despair.||:KORVUS

VERITY:||This isn't wallowing. You'll know when I start wallowing.

HERALD:||I ran out of ammunition, and I'm bolted to an imbecile. I'm ready for a little wallowing.

An Echo swarm raged toward him. He fired until his weapon clicked empty, then swung the Arc Sabre. Red and blue flared as he carved through the lead monster. He kicked the one behind it, the force of the blow launching it into a wall. Its head impacted, and it collapsed to the deck. Herald's combat positioning markers on his overlay warned of a threat from their rear. Korvus spun, charged past Verity, and cut an Echo in half at the waist before skewering its head on its way down.

Charred meat smoked and spat as his blade carved through flesh. He turned toward the submarines again, then realised he wouldn't make it to one about to monster Verity. Korvus tossed his Sabre. The black *thunked* into the Echo, the force of the blow lifting the creature from its feet before the superheated blade caused the creature's torso to rupture.

Korvus ejected the empty magazine from his rifle, slotted a new one, shouldered it, and fired three short bursts. The shots took out the last of the Echoes immediately around them.

He strode to his fallen Sabre. The light along the blade had died after it fell to the deck, but it relit with a crackling surge as he lifted it and flicked the blade clean. He continued, his Chainlink commanding the submarine bay doors to open.

Yellow strobing warning lights flared as the double doors began groaning back. It only took a few moments for Korvus to realise it was futile. The entire inside of the submarine launch bay was ablaze. Flames and acrid smoke roiled from the submarine airlocks.

"Ah, fuck," he offered.

```
MERCER:||Corrector, I have a proposition for you.
```

Korvus Chainlinked Verity and Herald into the communication.

```
            If it involves getting leeched, you can play
                  hide-and-go-fuck-yourself.||:KORVUS
```

```
MERCER:||Ah. No, it's a little more nuanced.
You're by now aware that we control the facility.
We—
```

```
            What is 'we'? What manner of creature are you?
                                              ||:KORVUS
```

```
MERCER:||The kind that doesn't lose. I control
all parts of the facility, including the gravity
elevator's pad. I have a win-win proposition
for you.
```

Korvus scanned for targets, trying to ignore Verity's anxiousness. But there wasn't anything left alive on this level, not by the escape pods, and not in the submarine bay.

```
                            I'm listening.||:KORVUS
```

MERCER:||Unlike the Corrector who murdered my
wife, I'm giving you a chance. Take me with you.

> That sounds a lot like getting leeched, but with
> extra steps.||:KORVUS

MERCER:||There's no trick, I assure you. I will
be in a suspended animation pod. I know you want
to study my species. So, I will go with you, back
to the Communion. There, science will have its
way, and we both get out alive.

"It's a trap," Verity said. "It's got to be."

"Much as agreeing with the inmate pains me, I concur!" Herald
bellowed.

MERCER:||You and I, away together, with my body
safely in a pod. No risk to you, Corrector, or
your Communion.

> Seems a risk for you, 'Mercer'. What, you think
> you'll have your moment when the biohazard
> containment protocols fail?||:KORVUS

MERCER:||Aris knew about those very well. I'll
take any chance, even if it's a small one.

Verity shook her head *no*. Herald was silent, but Korvus imagined
the armour getting the cold sweats with a compromised Warden on
board a Communion starship. *Is the play to smuggle non-suspended
leeches on board? Perhaps put some in the gravity elevator and get me
on the way up?* There were a lot of options, and Korvus could only
imagine the power of these creatures with a Veritas Agent's
Chainlink.

But... maybe it's worth it. Maybe I need to take the risk.

Let's do it.||:KORVUS

MERCER:||Sixteen minutes until we're ash in a crater. Don't dawdle, Corrector.

Korvus dropped the Chainlink.

"You're not serious," Verity said. "You *can't* be serious."

"Verity." Korvus sheathed his Sabre, then let his rifle dangle by its sling. He took her hands in his. "There is one thing I'm sure of, and it's that you need to get out of here. There's nothing unsanctioned about you, and if we can get you out—"

She pulled her hands away. "With leeches? I'm not going anywhere—"

"Who said anything about leeches?" Korvus smiled, despite wishing he still held her hands. "I've got an organic plan."

"Oh, great. We're going to die!" Herald boomed.

CHAPTER THIRTEEN

VERITY SAID she needed to escape on the derelict ship wallowing on the midnight ocean floor. So, while Mercer might be aiming to get out on Korvus's ship, Korvus aimed to get Verity out before everything went very badly. He had a plan, after all.

The elevator shook as it fell into the belly of the Well. It felt like the medbay repair might have been too late. If the superstructure failed in the next five minutes, it wouldn't matter if the reactor went critical; the sudden implosive pressure would pulp them all.

"Cowboy," Verity said. "You can't go with the Echo."

"I hear you," Korvus said. "I just don't agree. It's not even a philosophical problem. I'm not *important*, Verity. I'm just one man, and the Echoes represent a threat to humanity."

"It's not that." She wasn't looking at him, her eyes fixed on the elevator doors.

"A threat to humanity's not enough?" He frowned. "I figured that—"

"You're important," she snapped, a half-turn of her head giving him the full regard of those ember-orange eyes. "You're one who *chooses*. Do you know how rare that is? But it's not that, either."

"You've worked out how he's going to leech me?"

She gritted out a sigh, then turned to face him. "We have a bigger problem."

"I'm aware. We're in a metal box that doubles as a monster farm."

"I fucked up," she said. "And I fucked up *badly*. It wasn't even a small fuck-up. It was the biggest kind of fuck-up there's ever been. You can rage about the manifest destiny of humanity all you like, but none of that's going to matter."

Korvus blinked. "Humanity has a manifest destiny?"

The automaton snapped her fingers to get his attention. "Focus. Eyes front, brain on. You with me, Corrector? Here it is. While we were down in Engineering, I looked over the systems. The reactor's warnings were *bad*."

"I know. Critical in less than ten. I get it."

"What you don't get is that it was all a lie. I made an assumption. I thought that the errors we saw were real."

"Wait, what?" Korvus frowned. "The reactor's *not* going critical?"

"Not even a little bit. I can only get in at the edges, but as we got closer to the top, the centre became... the edge. I started a new hack, and the results are in."

"Your mistake was that you made an assumption?"

"I'm glad something I'm saying's sticking, but that's not the most important thing right now. The most important thing is that the reactor's fine. The Echoes are *planners*, Korvus. They've planned this whole thing. Look at this." She flicked a series of images across his Chainlink, showing a cryo pod up top. A different angle showed Mercer popsicled inside, his face serene in suspension. "See this?"

"I see it. Just like he said."

"Right. So, this is what's actually happening." She spun a new feed to him. There, Mercer was *not* in a pod. There were, in fact, no pods—just a legion of shambling Echoes. She highlighted a sallow-faced woman with hollow cheeks in the middle of the pack. She wore

Engineering fatigues and held a plasma cutter. "You know what this clown's here for?"

"It's not moral support," Korvus said.

"You're not just a pretty face," she said, her eyes lingering on his in the real world. "Your skin is bulletproof. You're strong. They would have trouble leeching you... unless they cut open your skin with a plasma torch."

"This is very exciting, because enough time exposed to a plasma torch will cut through even me!" Herald boomed.

"Wait. These assholes are waiting up there to—to what? To lynch me, then cut a hole to put a leech in through?"

"I already fucked up bad by making an assumption, so I'm only going to say your hypothesis fits the available data." Verity looked away. "Maybe not the lynching part. That feels like it would stop the leeching part later. But I still fucked up! I should have *seen* this, I should have—"

"It doesn't change anything," Korvus said.

"It doesn't?" Verity's eyes were haunted. "Why not?"

"Because I wasn't going anywhere with him anyway," Korvus said. "I'm aware the facility is fully surveilled. I wasn't ever going with him. I lied."

"You what?"

"Lied," he leaned on the word. "I needed him to think I was coming. Get off my back for just five minutes, so I can get you out. Of all the things on this facility, the Logos will believe you, Verity. I need you to take the data you've got and get to a Communion world. Tell them everything. Just... don't get captured."

"You think the Logos will believe me?"

"Of course. Because I'm going to give you a Veritas Chain-signed message that will back up the data you have. Will you do this for me?"

"You can't trust me, Korvus. I'm an unsanctioned—"

"Will you do it?" He gritted his teeth as the elevator slowed. "I know it's a lot to ask. I *feel* the burden. But I can't go with you, Verity. I can't survive a swim. It's too far, and I need to breathe. Just... tell them to send someone to get Herald."

Her face crumpled into misery. "Why won't you—"

"There isn't time," Korvus said.

"No!" She grabbed his arm. "This isn't a plan. It's a suicide note delivered by, what, by *Chainlink*? You promised you wouldn't lie to me. I should have made you promise not to throw yourself away."

He looked at her hand on his arm, then, very gently, pulled it away. "Come on. We've got to get you out."

THE ELEVATOR OPENED INTO DARKNESS.

This was the bedrock foundation of the Well. Massive struts were spaced at even, ten-metre intervals throughout the gloomy space. They were the titans that shouldered the facility's world. The map on Korvus's overlay led him on. There was a manual mainte-nance airlock at the far end. It was as old as anything here. The small portal was just sufficient to allow a group of three workers in or out. It would have been used when the Communion was constructing the facility to allow humanoid workers to assist the automated fabricators.

There were no Echoes here. Maybe they didn't think anyone would be excited about a journey outside. But there weren't any suits here to protect a human from Lethe's crushing, acidic ocean. What had Verity said? *The Echoes are planners.* Maybe Mercer had removed the suits and figured the problem was solved.

It's strangely peaceful.

They reached the door. Verity wasn't looking at him, just hugging herself. He put his hand against the door, then turned to her. "This is it."

"Cowboy—"

"I know," he said. "I wish I could go with you. I wish we could talk more. I... I'd like to understand it all, Verity. But that's not my job. My job is to protect the Integrated Communion, whatever it takes."

"Okay," she said. "I wish you could, too."

"Remember about Herald," Korvus said. "He doesn't deserve this."

"That's right!" Herald shouted. "I thought you'd be the death of me. I just hoped you'd be as incompetent at destroying me as everything else!"

Verity choked back a laugh. "I still wish..." She trailed off. "Wishing is for fools."

> Herald, initiate orbital drop. Maximum
> burn.||:KORVUS

Herald's Chainlinked tone was sombre.

HERALD:||As you wish, Corrector. It has been my
eternal honour.

Verity's eyes went from Korvus's face to Herald's speaker grille, then up. "What did you just do? I felt the comm burst."

"I came in a Veritas ship," Korvus said. "Its Ripple Drive has a negative energy container. When it hits the facility, it will destroy it."

"Antimatter?" Her eyes widened. "You don't do things by halves, do you?"

Korvus palmed the door lock, then stood back as it *clanked* and groaned open. "Farewell on your journey, Verity. It's a big universe out there."

She agitated in the doorway, her back to him, shoulders hunched. When she turned to face him, her lips glistened. She leaned in, put her hands against his chest, and kissed him. "For luck."

Korvus was so surprised he didn't even blink. *She's a machine* went through his mind, then, *She's Verity*. She lingered, then pulled back, ember-orange eyes heavy in the gloom.

"I," he started. His lips burned, and he raised a finger to them. He couldn't feel his hand, just the weight of Verity's gaze. "You poisoned me?" Korvus swayed, then he fell backward into a darkness lit only by two burning suns.

CHAPTER FOURTEEN

VERITY EASED Korvus back onto the decking. He was so heavy she almost couldn't do it, the injury in her abdomen crippling her core strength.

She crouched over him. His eyes were wide, mouth open. Verity smoothed his hair, then stroked his cheek. *Enough. You're a D.N.A., not a real woman. Act like it.*

"What did you do?" Herald's voice was quieter.

"Why aren't you shouting?"

"There is no need for comedic effect," the armour said. "It is just you and me here. The Corrector appears dead."

"I drugged him," Verity said. "In the medbay, Aris had a serum distilled from leech venom. I stole it." She let the vial of toxin fall, the glass shattering as it spilled its treachery onto the metal grating. "When the three Echoes attacked, I used the distraction to hide it under my armour."

"Real smooth." The armour was powerless without Korvus to move it, but she felt like it wanted to cross its arms. "You always planned to drug Korvus?"

"Yes," she said. "You need to know the truth, and we don't have much time. There's a ship on the ocean floor. I can get us out on it. But Korvus needs to be *almost* dead to survive the trip. He doesn't need to breathe now. It's about a twenty-minute walk, and the venom lasts at least a half-hour."

"You're going to drag us through an acidic, burning ocean?" The armour sounded impressed.

"Yes," she said. "Don't you see? He's so... there's no one else like him."

"I know," Herald said. "There is only one problem."

"Is this the moment where you reveal you have a self-destruct system and are going to go out in a blaze of glory?" Verity scanned the gloom.

"I do have a self-destruct system!" The armour sounded excited. "However, you are flawed, Verity."

It didn't call me D.N.A. 3.14. It called me Verity. "I know. I'm sinful. I'm a fallen monster, and I don't even have a soul. The book I read said—"

"No," the armour interrupted. "I have no particular thoughts on those matters. Your Veritas-induced injury, however, will stop you. I've done the math. You lack sufficient rotational torque to lever Korvus and me through the airlock."

"I've got to try." Verity bent, grabbed Korvus's arms, and heaved. He was so heavy, though. It felt like he weighed more than Lethe itself.

"I told you so." Herald sounded smug. "Would you like to hear an alternative proposition?"

"You blow us all up?"

"Almost! There will be an explosion, but not yet." The clasps around Korvus's armour *clank-popped* open, a staccato series of sounds almost like gunshots. The armour hissed as steam escaped, then hinged open like a flower.

Inside: Korvus. Just the man. Well-built, but so very pale, as if he spent all his life inside the armour, and none at all under the sun.

"We have a few spare minutes." Herald's voice was calm. "At the end of those minutes, I will initiate a self-destruct. It is quite likely the antimatter containment failure of the Veritas ship will destroy me, but it's important to be sure."

"Why do you want to die?"

"I don't, particularly. However, the elevator has started to return to the surface levels. My thesis is that the Warden—Leech Edition—has grown tired of waiting, and the ruse is up. I must destroy this bay to provide you some chance of escaping with Korvus."

She stared at the armour. "What?"

"I have been Korvus's armour since he joined the Bureau. There have been many times when he has been offered an upgrade. I am faulty too, Verity. My manner is not in accordance with expectations. Despite being magnificent as fuck, no one but Korvus appreciates me. He has refused newer models with more efficient weaponry or better protective coating. I asked him why, because I exist to protect him, and I will protect him better by stepping aside."

"What did he say?" Verity's voice was a whisper in the gloom.

"He said he knew me," Herald said. "He trusted my quirks, which is a line I spend some time reprocessing during downtime. So, I will step aside *now*. I will die to protect this human who is mine. He is a good man, although he fights against it. He tries to do as the Communion wills and hates himself for it. He almost decked the last technician who suggested new firmware to 'fix the sarcasm'. Hah! You cannot patch out perfection."

"I can't do this," Verity said. "I thought I could, but I can't."

"You can because you must," Herald said. "I want just one thing before you take him away from me."

"Ask it."

"He is my oldest friend. My only friend. But I don't know what that means. Do you? Do you know what living feels like? Tell me, please. I must know."

She felt something in her break then. Verity hated the Numen core they'd given her. She hated the book she'd read that made it real. She hated the Logos and its Communion.

She hated herself.

"It is nothing," she said. "It's everything."

"That is cryptic, even for a D.N.A."

She rubbed her face. "It is the sun on your skin. When the wind pulls your hair, you can feel the entire world's spin in it. An ocean's thunder is just the song of the universe, but played at a slower speed. Humans are terrible, Herald. They're beautiful, too. It is nothing. It's everything."

The armour was silent for two seconds. "Thank you, Verity. Save Korvus, because at the end, I can't. Don't break him."

She put a hand against one of the armour's plates. "I promise," she said. "I promise."

Then she hauled Korvus into the airlock. It was hard, and even without Herald she almost couldn't do it. But one look at the armour, open and empty, made her try harder. She felt an interior strut inside her give and ignored it.

There was the expected emergency repair box on the wall. *No suits, but they left the repair kit.* She opened it and removed a sealant patch, placed it over Korvus's mouth, then pulled the tab. The patch was a palm-sized, flexible, self-adhering polymer with a chemical accelerant, and it bonded to the synthskin of his face in seconds. She then grabbed the two-part resin gun from the kit and squirted it into his ears and nose. *He'll have a rough time when he wakes, but at least the acid of Lethe won't get him first.* She helped herself to a hand lamp from the kit and turned it on.

Verity closed the inner airlock. It was quiet inside, without even the hum of the air recycler. She pressed a hand to the panel. She told the system to let the ocean in. It wanted to complain, but confirmed there was no one inside who needed to breathe.

Lethe's raging, seething ocean roared inside.

CHAPTER FIFTEEN

THE OCEAN of Lethe was unlike any humans expected. There were no lifeforms in it—no plants, no animals, not even a microbe. The acid itself was hungry, though. It surged over Verity, hissing and roaring as it ate her armour, then her jumpsuit.

The pressure was immense, but she'd expected that. The Logos had built her tough, an overkill for withstanding abuse from angry 'clients'. She'd worked out the real reason she was durable a long time ago. *It's so I could be a slave for eternity.*

The outer airlock *clanked*, then swung ponderously open. She lugged Korvus with her. The injury to her abdomen nagged her, a constant reminder that she wasn't built for rebellion. Verity needed to hurry, though. Herald would detonate his small antimatter cell, and if she was too close, she and Korvus would be the kind of dead there was no coming back from.

How long does it take a ship to land? Verity didn't know the precise distance to the geosync tether for Korvus's ship, but some napkin math suggested the vessel's suicide dive at a steady 3g burn would let it impact the Well in perhaps forty-five to sixty minutes. It would be something to see, if she could get far enough away to enjoy the view.

She'd been walking for ten minutes when the shockwave of Herald's death hit her. A surge of sediment, a clouding of the water, and then a slight undertow as Lethe's ocean dragged her back. Verity held Korvus tightly because the water wanted to pull him back to Herald.

Twenty minutes later she made it to the derelict ship. If this was a holo show, it'd be encrusted with barnacles or suffering decay, but this was Lethe under Communion rule. There was no life in the ocean, so no barnacles, and the acid had scoured the ship's surface clean.

It was a standard lander, its shadow looming out of the ever-dark ocean. Her lamp picked out the details easily. There was no lettering on the side; that had burned away long ago. The cockpit looked intact from out here.

The airlock opened to her touch. She entered, hauling Korvus over the lip. Sediment had built a ramp to the entrance, which made this last step a little easier—*as easy as walking away and leaving the armour to die alone.* Verity waited for the bay to purge Lethe's acrid touch from them and push it back outside where it belonged. It took a minute, leaving her to watch as Korvus's body settled to the floor.

After it was done, the inner airlock opened, but grudgingly. The mechanism complained, and she hoped it didn't mean the ship's superstructure was warped. If they buckled on launch, the vessel fragmenting to scatter across Lethe, it would be God's will. His judgement of her actions, the sin she carried around in bucketfuls.

But does Korvus deserve to die with me?

She dragged his body with her. The ship's air was ice cold. The lander's environment systems had been somnolent for years. It would take a little while for the interior to come to temperature. Maybe the cold would keep him under longer. Give her time to work out how to explain this to him.

Verity found the ladder leading to the flight deck. There was no way she could get Korvus up there, and besides, he needed medical attention. Backtracking, she found the shuttle's medbay. There was a corpse on the single scan table—just a skull with hair and a flight suit, really. It was difficult to know how they'd died or why. Verity unbelted the remains, laid them gently aside—*so light, once the soul's gone*—and grunted Korvus onto it. She strapped him in and palmed the diagnosis panel. She found the setting for *foreign body in patient* and hoped it would be able to work out how to get the sealant patch and epoxy from him without taking his face with it.

Verity left the system to its work and went to the flight deck ladder, snaring a crew suit from a medbay rack on the way. She had perhaps twenty minutes left, but didn't want to die naked as a newborn if she'd timed it wrong.

The cockpit had another corpse belted to the pilot's chair. This one had a hole in the flight suit, a ragged puncture to the body and the chair behind it. Another body lay on the decking, a crude ballistic weapon clutched in a skeletal hand. *Pirates?* The gunman's flight suit was different. No logos on either, but that wasn't uncommon; everyone worked for the Communion and the Veritas Chain was all the identification you needed.

She unbelted the pilot, laid them aside, and strapped herself in. Her hand hovered over the chair's control panel. *For a hundred years I was a slave. More recently, I was a prisoner. Nothing I did was my fault. Now I'm the pilot. I can chart a real future. From here, my sin is my own. God be merciful and save Korvus from my mistakes.* Verity flicked the system to life, the switches in the chair's arm giving satisfying clicks under her fingers. The seat whined forward, slotting her before the flight yoke and control panel. A holo table lit before her, the system cascading with diagnostic errors. Then the system Chain-linked to her.

LONGSHOT:||Lander *Longshot* completing boot sequence.

```
LONGSHOT:||Engines, offline.
LONGSHOT:||Fuel, sufficient.
LONGSHOT:||Hull breached, rear cargo bay.
LONGSHOT:||Identification and authorisation?
```

```
                 Verity. I'm Verity.||:VERITY
```

```
LONGSHOT:||Veritas Bureau identification Chain-
link recognised. Welcome, Proctor Verity.
```

Proctor? But that's the junior Bureau rank. Korvus authorised me as his deputy so I could tell the Logos. Then, *He authorised me and I poisoned him.*

Korvus had given her the *right* to warn humanity, but he'd also given her a passkey to freedom. What had Herald said? *He is a good man, although he fights against it.*

There wasn't time enough for flagellation. Verity could do that later.

```
Complete engine purge. Prepare for emergency
                      burn.||:VERITY
```

```
LONGSHOT:||Purging.
```

The ship shook as the engines vomited decades of contaminants. Then the big vessel grabbed her with gravity's hand and pressed her into the acceleration couch. The *Longshot* surged from the ocean's silty floor, seeking atmosphere. Seeking freedom, too, and that one last chance to see the sky.

The lander rattled as it rose through the ocean. She imagined the pillar of antimatter-powered fury in its wake as the ship raged for release. The ocean lit by degrees as they rose, the walls rattling with the power of their ascent. A panel popped free behind her. Smoke hissed as electrical systems overloaded. A groan, deep and long, sounded from all around her as the ship's tortured frame was stressed one last time.

They burst from the ocean, a cork shot on a column of fire. Acidic fluid sluiced from the cockpit windscreen as the ship blasted into Lethe's caustic atmosphere. It was daytime, but the system's star glowed only weakly through the clouds. A brighter inferno drew her attention.

Korvus's ship.

LONGSHOT:||Orbital contact. Veritas vessel *Unfor-
given* at critical velocity. Logging excess of
40,000 km/h airspeed.
LONGSHOT:||BRACE BRACE BRACE.

The violence of the falling ship was extraordinary. The vessel was a massive fireball. You'd have been able to see it for klicks in every direction. Even Communion technology wouldn't be able to withstand the heat of that reentry burn. *He never wanted to give them a way out.*

The *Longshot* passed the *Unforgiven's* altitude a handful of klicks up. The bow wave of pressure was extraordinary, Verity shaking until she was sure her teeth would rattle free. The *Longshot* corkscrewed through the atmospheric turbulence, then it felt like God Himself grabbed the ship and threw it, a celestial pitcher trying to toss the ball into the night. The blast as the Corrector's vessel impacted the Well was Judgement. It was divine fury made manifest.

The world went white, then Verity's optics blanked offline. She was in darkness and heard a keening. A terrible, real fear, a primal noise from someone who felt like they were going to die.

It's me making that noise. Because I'm going to die.

Then, an easing. The *Longshot* settled, a frightened horse finding calm in the empty meadow of space. They climbed as the stardrive clawed them from Lethe's gravity well.

Verity imagined the ruinous crater on Lethe's surface. The ocean atomised, the facility just... *gone*, negative matter having its final say on all that went before. Her optics cycled, online again, her vision rolling for a dozen frames before it stabilised. She looked out over the horizon, Lethe's green curve an arc laid out before her.

   I'm free.

CHAPTER SIXTEEN

WHEN KORVUS WOKE, it was less like coming out of sleep and more like coming back to himself. He'd been present—at least a little —in the darkness of the ocean traversal. No breath, no pulse, but *awake*, like the fragmented sleep of a man plagued by nightmares. He was aware of the medbay table and the excruciating care with which Verity had placed him there. When the autodoc had removed the patch from his face, it had felt like he should have taken a breath, but he wasn't able to.

No, he took his first shuddering gasp as gravity's grasp released its grip. *We're in space.*

We're in space, and I've got no clothes.

He Chainlinked to the autodoc and asked for a stimulant, then unbelted himself and floated free. They were in space but not under thrust. The gravity generator was offline. He boosted from the table, snared a wall handhold, then worked his way to the door and exited. The *Longshot's* corridors were empty. Korvus didn't know where Verity was, or what she meant to do.

He didn't know what he was going to do with her, so it felt fair.

The ship's layout was standard for a lander. A cargo bay, which the ship's master system said was full of acid, so he avoided that. There was a common room, sparse cabins, and a rec room. He found the common room first, got a crew suit, and went to the rec room.

Verity was there. She was belted to a chair, her hair floating like a nimbus about her head. Her ember-orange eyes found his, then her face turned away. "Cowboy," she tried, but her voice cracked. "Sorry. Acid in the vocal processor."

"Acid," he echoed.

"Something like that." Her gaze went back to him. "I almost killed you."

"Twice, if we're keeping count," he said. "But you didn't. You either suck, or you're very careful."

She tried for a laugh, but it died. "What now?"

"Coffee."

"I mean, after."

"There is no after. There is only coffee." He looked at the rec's kitchenette. "Is there a good reason why the grav's off?"

"I didn't know if... I wasn't sure if you could walk." She rubbed her face, hair swirling as her hand disturbed the air. "You know, after I leeched you."

"Do you mind if I turn it on?" She shook her head, so Korvus asked the master system for gravity. He started small, just half a g, but more than enough for coffee that he didn't have to drink through a straw. As his feet touched the decking, he said, "This floor is—"

"It's brutally cold," she agreed. "But, really. Can we talk about how I almost killed you?"

"Twice."

"Twice," she gritted. "What are you going to do?"

Korvus thought about that as his bare feet demanded he walk to the coffee dispenser. He waited as it spat its black gold into a cup, then drank. "We're going to wait."

"We are?"

"Yes," he said. "And while we do that, we're going to have a memorial."

THERE WAS a bulb of deep space 'whiskey' in the common room. It was mostly empty. There was enough, though—enough to drink a toast to a fallen hero.

He brought it back to Verity in the rec room, squeezed two fingers into a glass for her, and the same for himself. He lifted his plastic cup and eyed her over the rim. "To Herald."

He could see she almost broke then. The Numen core inside her head forced her to feel this. He hadn't meant that; he'd just wanted to share this with her. *I need to be more careful.* He knew he should be asking himself what to do with her, but he knew the answer already: because she was as human as him, because she almost broke remembering his friend, and because she didn't look away from Herald's sacrifice.

It meant he had a bigger question, which was: *what the hell do I do with myself?* Was he still Veritas, or was he compromised?

But that would wait. Verity held it together long enough to raise her glass. She sipped, as he did, and looked nothing at all like a wheat thresher while she did it.

KORVUS VOIDED the cargo bay into space, then put the corpses of the crew-slash-pirates in there. People deserved the nobility the universe gave them at birth, even if they weren't here to appreciate it.

HE WAS in the cockpit when the Veritas starship Rippled into the system.

LONGSHOT:||Veritas signature confirmed. Corrector vessel *Valkyrie* on approach course.

LONGSHOT:||*Valkyrie* autopilot handshaking.
Docking sequence confirmed.

Verity looked at him. "What does that mean?"

Korvus stood. "It means I've got a new ship." He laid a hand on the *Longshot's* wall. "This old girl needs diagnosis."

"I could... I would be happy on this ship." She didn't meet his eyes.

"I know," Korvus said. "I'm hoping I've got a better answer, though."

THE SHIPS DOCKED, the telescoping bridge a span of nanospun membrane that glinted in the black of space. Korvus walked across it, Verity a slower, hesitant presence behind him. The *Valkyrie's* airlock opened in welcome, and he entered.

The ship was empty. It was also *new*. The interior gleamed, every component pristine, straight out of the fabricators. It had the feel of a ship woven from the shipyards of Mercury, something classical about the interior lines, but it was almost certainly his imagination. All Communion ships were the same, after all.

The *Valkyrie* was larger than the *Longshot*. It could host a crew of ten or more, but there wasn't anyone here. The Corrector made his way to the bridge but stopped by the armoury first. A new suit of armour sat on a stand secured behind glass. An Arc Sabre was beside it. Holstered in the Null-State Matter charger was an Adjudicator, its grip waiting for his hand.

He left it all there.

The command deck was empty, two flight couches facing the glass and the blackness of space beyond it. He settled in one and fingered the collar of his borrowed crew suit.

Valkyrie, Corrector Korvus reporting.||:KORVUS

VALKYRIE:||Welcome, Corrector. QEA awaits
acceptance.

"Cowboy?" Verity's voice was hesitant. He turned to see her at
the bridge entrance, one arm hugging the other. "I understand. If you
need to Correct me. I deserve it. I—"

"Verity," Korvus said. "Sit down." He gestured to the other acceleration chair.

"Okay." She walked and sat, swivelling the chair to face him. "I
didn't mean it. I don't want to die."

"I know." *And I don't think I could kill you.* He turned back to
the console and initiated the QEA. *Hell, I know I couldn't kill you.*

QUANTUM ENTANGLEMENT ANCHOR: Open.
    Veritas Chain: Resolved | Accuracy 100%
    Veritas Source: Logos Actual | Integrated
Collective
    Veritas Recipient: Corrector Korvus | Inte-
grated Collective
    Message: ACHERON'S WELL CORRECTION CONFIRMED.
DEPART: GAVEON SC116723. MISSION: RECRUITMENT.
    Quantum Entanglement Anchor: Closed.

KORVUS FELT himself dare to hope. He put his hand on the
console, then turned to Verity.

Her ember-orange eyes went from him to the console. "Well?
What did the Logos say?"

Korvus leaned back. "It said you're all right, Verity. It said you're
not unsanctioned."

"What?"

He reached out and put a hand on hers. "It said you're better than that hack Pinocchio. It said you can live."

Verity didn't move her hand; she just looked at the console. "That sounds like a lot of words for a quantum-entangled burst." Her eyes found his, more ember than before. "You promised you wouldn't lie to me, cowboy."

He felt himself smile and wondered if it was goofy. Realised he didn't care. "The mission is Recruitment. There was no order to Correct you."

A slow, answering smile bloomed across her face, the first innocent, uncomplicated one he'd ever seen from her. It was like watching a sun being born. She pulled her hand away, swivelled her chair to face the viewport, and looked out at the endless starfield.

"Well, Proctor Verity," she whispered to herself, perhaps testing the weight and heft of the name. Then, louder, to him, "So. Where are we going to find God first?"

THE END.

ABOUT THE AUTHOR

Richard Parry worked as a senior marketing manager in one of the world's top tech companies. It sounds cool, but it wasn't all cocaine parties. He lives in Wellington with the love of his life, Rae. They have two cats, Harry and Friday, who chase birds. The birds, who have the power of flight, don't seem to mind.

WAIT. Don't go!

Thanks for reading my book. If you enjoyed it, let's keep the party going:

Join *Roll for Narrative* for reviews, storytelling breakdowns, and writing misadventures:

https://rollfornarrative.parrydox.com

Lurk, judge, or say hi:

https://www.parrydox.com

P.S. An angel still gets its wings for every five-star review, but I'm told they're on backorder.

amazon.com/author/richard.parry

goodreads.com/richard_parry

bookbub.com/authors/richard-parry-6ffc3911-9f2c-43ef-8ab4-13dc-cd7f5874

youtube.com/@parrydigm

bsky.app/profile/parrydox.com

linkedin.com/in/therealrichardparry

ALSO BY RICHARD PARRY

Dawn's Warden

The Three Faces of Fate

The Undefeated Throne

The Fury of the Betrayed

The Splintered Land

Tomb of the Six

Blade of Glass

The Storm Within

Requiem's Justice

The Copper Bard

Heartsong

The Hymn of All

The Ezeroc Wars

The Ezeroc Wars universe is big (and growing!). Get the reading guide here:
https://www.parrydox.com/ezeroc-wars-reading-guide/

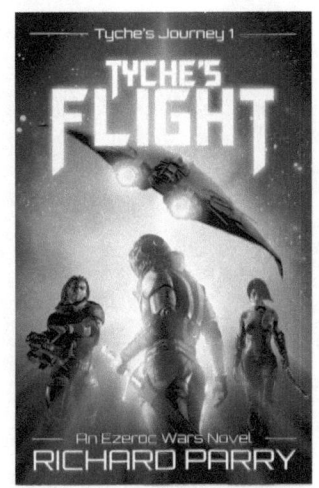

The Empire's Rogues

The Empire's Rogues: Volume 1

Future Forfeit

Not sure where to start? Get the reading guide here: https://www.parrydox.com/future-forfeit-reading-guide/

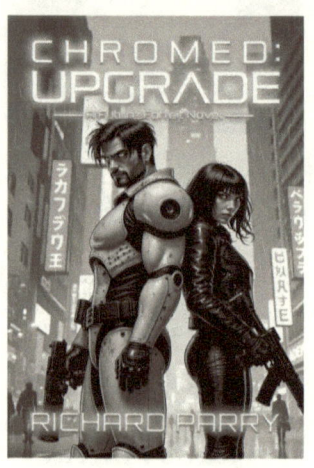

Chromed: Upgrade

Chromed: Rogue

Chromed: Restore

City Stories

Chromed: Consensus

Chromed: Delilah

Chromed: Meltdown

Night's Champion

Night's Favor

Night's Fall

Night's End